Cleaning the Slate

Andrea Warrilow

The first book in the series

At the Cliff Top

Cleaning the Slate

ISBN: 9798655649118

Independently Published

Printed by Amazon

First Edition

Acknowledgements

I would like to thank the following people for their help.

Firstly Paul, my husband, for being the "details matter" guy to my "It'll do" mindset. Also for getting his head around the formatting and uploading of this book. And, of course, being the inspiration for Caleb (maybe)!!!

Secondly Carola Rush for designing and setting up the lovely cover for the book.

Lastly, Leanne Regan and Christine Howson for patiently reading and reviewing the book before I embarrassed myself by letting anyone else see it.

Thank You xxx

Glossary of Terms

For those of you who don't 'do' horses, firstly don't panic, horses are a background, not the subject of this book. Secondly, I have used a few horse terms that might bamboozle you so I have explained them below in (slightly tongue in cheek) layman's terms.

Riding School - A place where people pay to be taught to ride, usually on horses owned by the school. Depending on the quality of the instruction, and the temperament of the horses it can be fun or terrifying, sometimes both.

Livery Yard - Place where rich horse owners pay someone to keep and look after their horses and do all the smelly, dirty jobs so the rich person can just enjoy riding them.

Liveries, Full Liveries - The horses kept at the above yard, full liveries are even ridden by the yard staff on days the rich owners don't want to ride them themselves.

Colic - A fairly common illness in a horses digestive system, that can kill them very quickly, sometimes despite the best efforts of a vet.

Bolt - When a horse is scared or feeling naughty and decides to run away/go home at speed, usually without the riders permission!

Trot - Horses pace. Faster than walk, a bit like jogging, can be bouncy and scary for a new rider.

Canter - Another pace. Generally faster than trot but less bouncy. More like running but not really fast. The fastest pace is gallop, which is what racehorses and bolting horses do.

Event/Eventing - A horse competition with 3 disciplines

1: Dressage - riding complicated moves in an empty arena - like dancing without music, except sometimes it does have music.

2: Cross Country - jumping lots of solid jumps, in the right order, over a long distance around fields, usually galloping between jumps. Jumps are mostly natural looking, unless they are sponsored by Land Rover.

3: Showjumping - jumping pretty coloured jumps, that are easily knocked down, in the right order, in an arena.

Event competitions can take place over one or three days.

Badminton - The most famous and prestigious three day Event in the UK.

Mounting block - Platform with steps that allows you to stand high enough to easily get on your horse.

Mare - female horse.

Gelding - male horse that has been castrated.

Cob - Small stocky horse, with strong legs.

Hand - Unit of measurement of horses height to the top of the shoulder. 1 hand = 4inches. No metric equivalent will be tolerated.

Series – At the Cliff Top

Book 1

Cleaning the Slate

"That Time"

Carrie was 32, happily married and living in a cute rural town. She had a great career and a plan to start a family soon, she had everything she wanted in life.

Who'd have thought a knock on the door could shatter her life into a million pieces? She knew, as soon as she opened the door to those two grave looking police officers, that her happiness had ended forever.

Looking back, after the funeral, she realised her whole life had been centred around Matt. Her parents were gone and she had no other family. He was her life. Without him, there was nothing left but an empty shell and grief – so much grief. She knew people survived losses like hers, she just didn't know how. How could there be any joy or wholeness ever again? Thank God there were no kids – Oh God, I wish there were kids, at least part of Matt would still be here.

He had been a wonderful husband, loving, kind, sexy, HERS. They had been together since forever and fitted each other like, well, a fitted thing.

How could one careless driver take all that away?

Oh Matt!

Chapter 1

Surviving

It was the morning of her first job interview, six months to the day after Matt's funeral. Carrie was a gibbering mess!

After months of blackness and grief, interspersed with therapy and self-help groups, she knew she had to move on. Carrie had been existing on her savings but it was time to re-enter the world, start trying to find a new normal, and a new income. She had tried going back to her old job, with disastrous results. Everyone was so kind and supportive at first but that just made her cry more. Colleagues, who she thought were friends, quickly started to avoid her, not knowing how to deal with her grief. She knew she could no longer be that career person, there was no drive to succeed any more. So after just three weeks, she left to find a new, simpler way of existing.

Having lost her parents in a car crash when she was in her early twenties, and then her husband, in the same way, seemed so cruel. Matt had been her rock when her parents died and for these recent months, it seemed that she was grieving for all of them. Her life had been back on track with Matt but now it was totally derailed.

"Good morning Mrs Jones and thanks for coming. I am Sally Walker, owner of Elver Livery Yard. I'm not good at this interviewing thing so let's just sit, drink coffee and get to know one another."

They entered a large living room with a great view of the stable yard and sat on saggy, comfy sofas. "So, I'm Sally and I hope I can call you Carrie?" Carrie smiled and nodded.

"I have to say it's a pleasant surprise to have an applicant for this job who is, umm, more mature. Most previous applicants have been young girls whose enthusiasm outweighs their ability! You do realise this isn't a well paid job?" Carrie nodded nervously. "I know I shouldn't try to talk you out of the job before we even start but I do want us to be honest with each other, and I don't want to waste your time if there has been some misunderstanding."

Carrie breathed deeply to steady her voice. "Yes I know what the pay is and I am still interested."

"OK, good." Beamed Sally and went on to explain the duties involved. She mentioned all the usual jobs Carrie was expecting, mucking out, cleaning tack, riding horses and everything else needed to run a livery yard. Carrie nodded her way through the list, trying to look confident.

Sally explained that the livery yard was about 85 acres, all grass and split into lots of small paddocks so horses could graze near each other but not all together. Mostly she split the horses into twos and threes, taking note of which ones got on well and which tended to fight a bit. Horses, like humans, don't always get on with each other and injuries could be caused if they had 'arguments'. She had stable spaces for twenty-four horses and only kept one of her own. All the others were paying guests. There was an outdoor riding arena with a special soft sandy surface where horses could be exercised as well as rides they could go on around the fields and out onto the roads. Some of the paddocks were used to grow hay in the summer to feed the horses in winter.

"How experienced are you as a rider Carrie?" Sally asked. Carrie explained that she had ridden since she was small and owned horses most of her life. She explained what local competing she had done and that she had trained a young horse in the past.

Sally noticed that Carrie became more eloquent when she talked about her horse experience. "OK, if it's alright with you, we'll take a couple of horses out for a hack in a while so I can see how you ride?" She continued, "While experience is good, I need to know that we can get on well together and I need someone I can trust. What can you tell me about yourself, maybe you can tell me why this is the right job for you at this point in your life?"

Carrie knew this would be where she blew it if she wasn't careful. She took a breath and told her story.

"Up to about six months ago, I was happily married, with a good career. Then my husband was killed in a car crash and I haven't really worked since. It has taken this time for me to rebuild my life and deal with the grief. I tried going back to my old job but the enthusiasm wasn't there. I need to do something different and find a new me. Being around horses is something I know, and something that gives me pleasure and a sense of well being." Carrie hoped Sally didn't see the tears on her cheek.

"Oh my dear, how hard for you," sighed Sally, "I don't think I would ever recover if I lost my Terry. I can see why you would avoid going back into a high powered career, but I do need someone reliable and physically strong. Do you think you're ready for this?"

"I'm sure I am," said Carrie. "I need to be busy and feel useful again."

Sally could see how hard it was for Carrie to talk about herself. She steered the conversation back to horses and they chatted happily for a while.

"Maybe I should tell you about my past?" smiled Sally. "It seems fair that we both share."

Carrie brightened. "I know you were an Event rider, I saw you go round Badminton once."

"Wow, you remember me!" said Sally. "I feel like that was a different lifetime." They chatted about eventing for a while.

Finally, Sally said, "Did you bring a riding hat? Let's go for a ride." They headed out into the yard and Sally showed Carrie around, introducing her to the horse she would ride.

"This is Sadie, she is an older mare and quite quiet. I am not testing you here, just getting a feel for your riding skills so I know how much I could ask you to do. I'm riding Bilbo, who is a bit of a hothead but very cute."

They fetched the tack and saddled their horses. Both animals were stabled and gleaming so Carrie guessed Sally had been busy before she arrived. As they led the horses to the mounting block Carrie racked her brains for an intelligent question to ask. "Do these horses belong to you or are they liveries?"

"Bilbo is a livery but Sadie is mine. I wouldn't put

you on someone else's horse till I see what you can do," winked Sally. "We'll ride through our fields so I can show you around, then we can head out onto the road for a circuit through the town."

Carrie was relieved, this was one thing she could do without tears or nerves. They mounted and headed out across the fields.

"It's great to be in the saddle again," said Carrie after a while. "I haven't ridden since I lost my old horse to colic about a year ago. We were thinking of starting a family so I thought I'd have a few years without a horse." She felt tears on her cheeks again and turned her head away.

"Let's canter up this hill and clear our heads," said Sally quickly. Sadie was cantering away before Carrie had even processed the thought. Carrie slowed her for a second to regain control then let her go and enjoyed the wind drying her face as they sped up the hill. Sally hung back and watched Carrie take control and then enjoy the canter. As they reached the top Carrie laughed and said, "Did you know she would take off as soon as you mentioned the 'C' word?"

Sally grinned, "I had an idea she might! And you passed the 'I'm not testing you' test with flying colours Carrie." They both giggled as they passed through a gate and out onto the road.

The route through the town was busy. Elver was not a big town but it had quite a few shops needing deliveries, a fair number of offices and a couple of small business type industrial estates. Big lorries and traffic jams were becoming more common. Both horses coped well with the passing traffic until a big lorry came up behind them, its air brakes hissing. Sadie was fine but Bilbo jumped and tried to spin round to see the approaching monster. Sally held him back but he bounced on the spot trying to bolt. Carrie reacted quickly, turning Sadie to stand between Bilbo and the lorry as it passed, Bilbo calmed as soon as Sadie was beside him. "Thanks," said Sally, "I was holding him OK but it was about to get messy! I always tense up a bit when I am on a customer's horse and something goes wrong – it's a big responsibility. You have good instincts in a tight situation."

Carrie smiled, "At least the lorry driver was thoughtful, passing us wide and slow, I hope he saw my hasty thank you wave."

As they rode back towards the yard Sally was quiet. Carrie had a feeling her tears had blown the interview and she felt very frustrated with herself. Being on a horse again felt so right and she could feel her stress drifting away. She knew there was no way she could afford her own horse now, or pay to ride at a Riding School. Maybe Sally would let her work for free in exchange for rides? But then how would she earn enough to feed herself? No – she needed a job and she needed to toughen up. If this wasn't the job she would find something else.

Once they got back and unsaddled the horses, Sally said, "I need to think before I make any decisions – can I call you later tonight?" Carrie agreed and went home to wait. She knew she had messed up. Who would want to rely on a woman who couldn't even chat for half an hour without blubbering! She slunk into her bedroom, lay down and ate chocolate, lots of chocolate. "What do I do now?" she thought aloud. "How do I move on when I can't even be normal around people?"

Matt, I miss you so much........

Chapter 2

Friendship

Carrie finally got up off her bed as she heard her housemates returning from work about 5.30pm. The whole afternoon had disappeared in a haze of grief and chocolate – again.

She had advertised her home for sharers, a couple of months after Matt's accident, as she couldn't bear to part with the house. Luckily the mortgage had been paid off by insurance after "that time", as she called the time of Matt's death.

The house was a 1940's, three-storey, detached house with a good garden and driveway in front, it matched all the others in the quiet cul-de-sac. The back garden had probably been bigger once but at some point, it had been sold off to build another road of houses behind. Now all they had was a big patio area. There were four bedrooms, an attic room and three bathrooms, along with a kitchen and living room. It was going to be their forever, family making, home.

The couple she found to share her house were

probably her salvation if she was honest. They were wonderful people, blessed with warmth and kindness.

A few curtains in the street twitched when two men moved in with her but, hey, it's fun to stir the old town up a bit!

The house was big enough for her and the lads to have their own spaces and still have a big kitchen and living room to share. It was unconventional but it really worked. Many evenings found the three of them chilling in the living room, watching TV or just chatting. David and Gregg were a great addition to her home and their rent paid most of the bills. If she was careful she did not need to earn a great deal to survive. She was so glad to know that they would never be interested in her in a romantic way, unlike the creepy single guy who was the first applicant for the house share, ugh!

The three of them often cooked meals together and shared the chores. They were more house proud than she was, so she never had to nag. Despite a good social life, they were a very devoted couple and had definitely grown out of the 'must go out every night on the pull' phase. She was really very lucky to have found them.

When she appeared from her room that afternoon Dave took one look at her and put the kettle on. "Bad day?" he asked. Carrie nodded and curled up on the sofa. Gregg gave her a kiss on the top of her head and said, "Wanna talk?" Carrie explained what had happened at her interview and how her afternoon had spiralled into a self-hate session.

"Maybe it wasn't as bad as you think?" said Dave, bringing tea. "It sounds like this Sally is a good judge of character – she let you loose on her horse pretty quickly and you handled that bit well. I bet she can see through the tearful bits and find the great person you really are. Wait for her call before you beat yourself up too much."

As Carrie finished her tea, already feeling a little better, her mobile started to ring. "OMG, OMG – answer it for me," she squealed. And then answered it herself.

"Hi, it's Sally at the livery yard. If you're still interested I would like to offer you the job, on a months trial, with a view to making it permanent after that. Can you start soon?"

"Wow, are you sure, I thought I'd blown it with crying like that!" gasped Carrie. Then she pulled herself together and said, "I would be delighted to take the job, and I can start tomorrow if you like?"

Sally laughed, "I am sure we'll get on very well if you stay that keen! I realise you're still a little fragile after your sad loss and I'm very happy to offer you a horse to cry on when you need it! As long as you can be reliable and work hard I can cope with the odd tear. Let's give it a try and re-evaluate in a month to see if we're both happy to carry on?"

Carrie thanked her, put down the phone and burst into tears. As the lads looked at her in confusion, she blubbed, "I have a job and I'm so happy."

They looked at each other as they hugged her and silently agreed that women were a mystery to them.

* * * * *

Over the next two years, Carrie and her boss Sally became firm friends as well as colleagues. It was a huge relief for Sally to find a mature worker. Usually by the time Sally had got a young girl trained to her standards the girl left, realising she could earn more money doing pretty much any other job. Carrie found Sally at just the right time for both of them it seemed.

The jobs on a livery yard were monotonous but Carrie was happy with monotony – no nasty surprises, she'd had enough of those. Each day consisted of feeding, turning horses out to graze, mucking out, bringing horses back into their stables, exercising some of the horses, as well as offering help and advice to any horse owners having issues. Obviously, there were always other jobs such as haymaking and tack cleaning to break the monotony, what a glamorous life!

Carrie loved the early mornings and the hard physical work, it was a great way to remain too tired to think. She loved exercising the horses for the full liveries. Her previous career had equipped her with good people skills, which helped her with awkward horse owners. All in all, it provided Carrie with everything she needed, except enough money to live well. As she did not feel like living well this wasn't an issue.

Sally was older than Carrie by a few years and owned the stables with her husband Terry. He managed to hold down a job in IT as well as being the handyman for the yard. Luckily he could work from home a lot and was quite practical. The poor chap often ended up mending fences or stables instead of sitting at his computer like a good IT chap should. Just as well he was a partner in the IT business so he could get away with it. Sally maintained that Terry would rather be covered in horse muck than sitting in a business meeting anyway, but that they preferred to have a safe wage coming in.

Sally herself had been quite a successful Event

rider in her teens and twenties, competing at some of the biggest events in the UK and Europe. She never really said why she left eventing, she could be breeding or training eventing horses now, but Carrie had a feeling there was a story of heartbreak there somewhere. Sally's riding skills far outshone Carrie's but Sally was very generous with her knowledge and had taught Carrie so much. Sally trusted Carrie to exercise all but one or two of the horses. Luckily Carrie was petite and lightweight so she could ride even the smaller ponies on the yard. The two worked side by side in comfortable efficiency and, apart from a couple of young Saturday girls, they ran the yard of twenty plus horses alone. Carrie found the work cathartic and looked forward to each day with something akin to her old love of life. Sally was easy to work for and their friendship had become another lifeline.

Sally was as practical and level headed as they come about most things in life, but she had one 'quirk' that was really out of character. She loved to follow celebrity gossip and any chance to 'celebrity watch' was her idea of heaven. A town like Elver did not exactly have a thriving celebrity scene so she made do with buying gossipy magazines and spent her evenings trawling the internet for juicy titbits. Carrie and Terry couldn't raise much enthusiasm for Sally's hobby but they both humoured her as best they could.

Every few months Sally got the urge to visit London and hang out in one of the celebrity hot spots, in the hope of seeing some of her heroes. Terry had long since put his foot down and refused to go with her but Carrie had agreed to go the last couple of times. Well, it was an outing, and a reason to scrub up and get girlie!

Knowing Carrie could not afford these trips and needing a partner in crime, Sally had bribed her that she would pay, how could Carrie refuse? This time they were heading to the famed Regency restaurant for a meal. The restaurant was known to attract the movers and shakers and Sally hoped that someone 'A list' would be there. The fact that the meal would cost more than Sally paid Carrie for a weeks work didn't seem to dull Sally's enthusiasm one bit. Terry was paying as her birthday gift – on the condition that he wasn't expected to go!

What have I got myself into Matt?

Chapter 3

That Meal

Carrie and Sally sat on Elver station waiting for the train to London. Sally was totally hyped and chattered on about who they might see that evening. Carrie tried to sound interested, she really wanted her friend to enjoy herself, but she quietly thought she would be glad when they were on the train home again. She hadn't even heard of half the celebrities Sally was talking about and she definitely wouldn't recognise them if they did appear.

"I am going to try and sneak a few photos if we see anyone good tonight," said Sally. "I'm sure I can do it without being obvious!"

Carrie was quite glad her own phone got dropped in a water bucket the previous week so she could not be pressed into being the photographer. Sally could be a bit embarrassing sometimes.

Sally was a natural beauty in her slinky black dress, with long legs, toned from years of riding, and a neat bob of auburn hair which never looked messy even when she took off her riding hat – so not fair!

Carrie always wished she had longer legs, hers were just normal for a petite 5'3" slightly curvy girl. She wore a deep purple dress that was flattering without standing out. Carrie liked to hide these days. Her hair was dark and wavy, and usually in a ponytail out of the way, often adorned with hay and never really tidy. She had it loose tonight as it formed a bit of a barrier to hide behind when she was outside her comfort zone. Sally said it looked wild, sexy and mysterious but Carrie only heard the wild part and felt a bit self-conscious as the train arrived and the hour's journey began. When they reached Liverpool Street station there was a taxi waiting to take them to the restaurant – good old Terry, keeping his wife safe and sound.

The Regency had obviously had a long and up-market history. It was a fine building with columns and arches along the street. Once inside they were greeted by a very snooty waiter who asked for their names and consulted his bookings. Carrie felt out of place and very judged. As the women stood waiting they surveyed the room, Sally with excitement and Carrie with slight trepidation. She was hoping Sally wouldn't embarrass herself if she saw someone famous. The dining room was opulent, if slightly tired looking, with red velvet curtains and dark oak furniture. Sally went into raptures imagining all the famous bums that had sat on the velvet cushions over the years. The thought made Carrie squirm a little but she kept smiling.

The waiter seemed to be taking ages finding their booking – considering Sally had booked it months ago. Finally, after some hushed but angry discussions with another waiter, the snooty man came back to them, all false smiles and sliminess. "Sorry for the delay ladies, please follow me." He led them right to the back of the restaurant to a long table that wasn't even set for dining. The four chairs were pushed deep under the table and there were no place settings. To be honest, it didn't look like the table had been used for ages, there was no table cloth and the candles in the middle were dusty and half burnt. The waiter quickly pulled out two of the chairs facing the wall and disappeared stating he would get some cutlery.

"Well," said Sally, "that was strange, and a bit rude. I'm not sitting looking at a wall all evening." Carrie agreed and they quickly pushed the chairs round one end of the table where Sally, at least, had a good view of the room. Whilst they waited for the waiter to return Sally studied all the other guests, just in case. Within a couple of minutes, she was wriggling with excitement and whispered, "Over there Carrie, on the right, three tables away – it's Carl from EastEnders!" Carrie never watched EastEnders but the guy did look a bit familiar. Sally carried on searching the room but seemed disappointed that 'Carl' was her only find.

"Oh well, the evening's young yet," said Carrie, "I

expect there will be others in later. I hope this waiter appears soon, I need a drink."

After another 15 minutes, Carrie was getting really cross. "Where is that snotty waiter? I bet he wouldn't keep Carl from EastEnders waiting like this!" Sally was still happy scanning the room. Her voice was preoccupied and vague when she answered, "I expect he'll be back soon."

After another 10 minutes, Carrie had had enough. "I'm going to the bar to get us drinks and shout at someone," she said as she left the table.

"Hmmn," said Sally not even looking her way.

When Carrie reached the small discreet bar at the front of the room a different waiter was there. With relief and some anger, she said, "Excuse me but we have been seated, then totally ignored by our waiter and we're hungry and thirsty. The table isn't even set for us yet and we've been here nearly 30 minutes. I thought this was a high-class restaurant, you certainly charge enough."

The guy looked at her in horror and started to apologise profusely, "Let me take a drink order madam, on the house of course, and I will see who is responsible for keeping you waiting." Carrie was quite proud of herself for her bravery and she ordered her drinks with a little smile on her lips. This waiter could not have been nicer – and he was hot! "Oh wow, where did that thought come from?" she asked herself. It had been a long time since she had noticed cute guys. Not that there was any chance of her wanting one, she had had the love of her life and anything less would be like making do.

Carrie turned to go back to their table, having thanked the cute waiter, glad to get away from the feelings that had stirred. As she passed the door of the restaurant it opened and two men walked in, chatting away. She supposed she should check they were not hugely famous for Sally!

As she sneaked a peek at them, they turned towards her. Her mouth fell open and she let out a little squeak. "Stephen Barratt – is that really you?" she squealed, rather louder than she intended. The guy looked up hearing his name and stared at Carrie for a minute. She could see the cogs whirring then, thankfully, his face lit with recognition and he reached out to her. "Wow, Carrie Smith, you haven't changed much!"

He turned to his companion and said, "Caleb, this is Carrie, we were at college together." Carrie looked at Caleb and got the 'Cute Guy' feeling for a second time that night. She also got the impression she should know who he was, but couldn't grasp the thought.

She turned back to Stephen and said, "So, how are you? what are you doing now? Did you carry on with your nerdy electronics stuff or did something else grab you?" Stephen started to answer when Carrie started again, "Ooh are you still with Ellie? I remember thinking you two would always be together but that was so long ago?"

Stephen laughed and said, "Same old Carrie, never stops to breathe, and yes, Ellie and I have two kids and I'm still into electronics, but in the film industry now, hence my illustrious friend here."

Carrie squealed, "Ooh Ellie-bee..... and kids, wow! And film industry, cool, I'm here with my boss, she'd love to talk to someone in films, and .... hang on.........your friend.........OMGOMGOMG....!"

Carrie was finally silenced when she looked properly at the second man with dawning recognition. "You're Caleb Kirkmichael aren't you?" she almost whispered. The two men laughed and nodded.

Caleb finally managed to get a word in as he shook her hand. "Usually it's me that has the pretty girls throwing themselves at me in public, I don't know whether to be glad or hurt that you ignored me and hero-worshipped my special effects guy instead. It is nice to meet you Carrie. It sounds like you and Stephen have some catching up to do, so I will get us a table whilst you chat."

Caleb Kirkmichael was about as 'A list' as any celebrity could be. He stormed to fame in his early twenties in Hollywood fast action movies, playing the young sidekick in a franchise of movies about espionage and car chases – not Carries thing. You would have to be in a coma not to know about him though. Since then he had done so may box office smash movies that Carrie couldn't even remember half of them. As he got older the roles changed but he was always good to watch and anything with him intended to go straight to the top. He was versatile too – she'd seen romances and even a Sci-fi film with him in. He was often on the news, both for film publicity and for his support of animal welfare charities in America. He was tall and lean but she suspected he had a pretty good group of muscles under his shirt. His eyes were a dark mahogany and they seemed to see right inside you when he was on screen, making him a great leading man. There was always the odd scandal and juicy story, but that was Sally's area, not Carrie's.

How could she not have recognised him? Sally would be ashamed of her. Oh God – Sally! She glanced across and saw Sally happily sitting and watching 'Carl'. Phew, she probably hasn't even realised I've gone, thought Carrie. Caleb Kirkmichael went off laughing to find a waiter but Carrie was still mortified she did not recognise him at first. "Have I offended him Stephen? I know Hollywood types can be a bit self-important."

Stephen was still smirking as he answered. "Hell no, Caleb is too mature and too successful to be a diva, but he'll dine out on that story for years!"

"Phew," said Carrie, "I'd hate to spoil his mood. I hope he has better luck getting a table than we did. We've been given the equivalent of the naughty table, stuck up the back facing the wall. No one has even been near us to take an order!"

"That's not good, but they'll know who Caleb is even if you don't, he **will** get a table," he laughed.

"I hope they don't give him our table, they seem to have forgotten we exist," joked Carrie. "Ooh maybe you could join us, it would be great to catch up and there's plenty of room, or do you need privacy?"

"Let's see if we can sort this," said Stephen, grabbing her hand and wandering over to where Caleb was chatting with the snotty waiter from earlier.

Caleb laughed at something as they approached and the waiter's prim face broke into an obsequious smile. When the waiter noticed Carrie was with Stephen and Caleb he did a double take, looking slightly less snooty than before. Caleb started to say that there would be a short wait for a table when Stephen said, "How about we share Carrie's table, she says it's big enough?"

Looking pointedly at the waiter he said, "That might mean these ladies finally get the service they deserve from the Regency, I know how a famous face improves your mood Mr Alvers." Caleb looked pleased with the idea and agreed. Mr Alvers, who according to his badge was the manager, finally dropped the snooty look and beetled away calling for his staff.

"This is a great idea!" said Caleb. "As long as your boss won't mind Carrie?"

Knowing how excited Sally would be sharing a table with Caleb Kirkmichael, Carrie didn't feel the need to consult her. "Have you been filming some-thing today?" asked Carrie.

"We've been working on a special effect needed for filming next week – it did not go well," laughed Stephen. "We decided a drink and a decent meal was deserved after a day of failures."

Carrie, Caleb and Stephen approached their table just as Sally returned from the ladies room. As she sat she looked around for any new celebrities to ogle. She saw Carrie coming and smiled, looked beyond her, and her eyes widened in shock! Carrie grinned and sat in her seat just as Caleb and Stephen grabbed the other two seats and the waiters arrived with tableware. "Sally, may I introduce Stephen and Caleb, who will be dining with us." Sally's face was a picture – she didn't know where to look or what to say she just grinned and fanned her face with the newly arrived menu. Carrie whispered in her ear, "Happy Birthday Sally!"

After the food orders were placed Carrie and Stephen carried on with their catching up whilst Sally and Caleb chatted away about the film industry. Despite Carrie's initial concerns, Sally appeared to be her usual unflustered self and, if she was star-struck, she was hiding it well. Stephen was happily talking about his wife Ellie and their kids. He and Carrie compared notes about their other friends from college and what they were doing now.

The food arrived and the conversations slowed, the meals really were wonderful. Every now and then Carrie would look up at Caleb and Sally to check if their conversation was flagging but they seemed fine. She did notice that each time she looked up Caleb seemed to be looking at her, but she guessed he was just checking his friend was not being bored to tears by her.

She tuned back into Stephen just as he said, "What about you Carrie – did you stay with that guy you met in our last term? Matthew, or something, I think?" Carrie's world suddenly turned a somersault – she knew the question was going to come – she thought she was prepared but WHAM! Before she could control her face, or even begin to answer, she felt tears on her cheeks and a lump the size of a tractor in her throat. She didn't know what to do, should she rush for the loo? Should she brazen it out – say she was choking on her dinner? Stephen was eating and hadn't looked up, Sally was so engrossed in Caleb's story she hadn't heard the question. She desperately tried to stop the tears and swallow the huge 'blub' that threatened to burst out – probably with snot bubbles and everything.

Just as she thought she would burst she felt a strong arm on her shoulder and saw a tissue thrust towards her hand. She turned in surprise as she buried her face in the tissue. Caleb had somehow dashed around the table and found her a tissue in about a nanosecond. As she turned to him he took her in a gentle hug and said nothing, just let her breathe, and probably snot on his shirt! Sally followed his movements and suddenly realised what was happening. She took Carrie from Caleb and held her tight. Stephen was beside himself for upsetting her and still didn't know what he'd said. While Carrie recovered Sally filled them both in on Matt's death. After a few seconds, Carrie got herself back together and started to apologise for her behaviour.

Everyone was a bit uncomfortable for a few moments, then Caleb became her rescuer a second time when he took on the conversation. He amused them all with tales of filming to break the ice and take the attention away from her tears. Carrie sat and quietly listened while she got her voice back under control. He really was a good storyteller, she was laughing again by the end of his story. Once again Caleb seemed to be looking at her as he spoke, probably keeping an eye on the fruit-loop, she thought. But it felt OK.

As the evening went on they seemed so relaxed it was as if they were all old friends. Carrie had to pinch herself, this wasn't what they had planned but it was so good. Sally had a tale to beat any of her other celeb-stalking tales and Carrie had met someone who remembered her from before she got broken. It was the first time she had looked back into her past since "that time" and it felt good, despite the tears.

With a sudden yelp Sally jumped up, looking at her watch, "Carrie we must fly or we'll miss the last train." Carrie grabbed her bag and moved to say her goodbyes to Stephen and Caleb.

Both men were a bit surprised and Caleb looked a bit confused. "I'm not used to relying on trains," he said, "don't they run all night?"

Sally laughed, "Not these days, especially if you live outside the capital."

He thought for a minute then said, "Stay, we're enjoying each others company and my driver can take you home later." Sally looked at Carrie and laughed.

"We can't ask you to take us home, it's an hour's drive each way. And we have to work in the morning, we'd better get moving, but thanks for the offer."

Caleb looked a bit crestfallen and said, "What if we carry on our conversation in the car, that way we can enjoy your company for longer and enjoy the drive too?" Carrie shrugged, leaving the decision to Sally, she'd already planned to stay at Sally's for the night so no one would be worrying about her.

Sally made a pretence of considering then said, "OK let's stay – if you're sure you don't mind giving us a lift? I'll text Terry and tell him not to wait up." Caleb looked really happy at her decision and called a waiter for more coffee. Carrie wondered why he was so keen to keep them there but she was quietly pleased too.

They resumed their group conversation with Stephen describing some of the stranger special effects he had been asked to rig up. Eventually, the restaurant emptied and they took the hint that it was time to move on. The girls wandered to the front of the restaurant to pay, only to find that their tab was already covered. Caleb just smiled and looked a bit embarrassed. "I can put it down as a business expense," he said quietly and refused to discuss it any more.

They left the restaurant and entered a pub next door for one more drink. Carrie and Caleb ended up shoulder to shoulder in the crowded bar and they chatted away about this and that. Caleb was definitely a gentleman, he wanted to know all about Carrie's job and her life. He was careful to skirt around her bereavement. He told her about his life, his family in America, and how he was beginning to tire of the Hollywood lifestyle and yearned for something a bit more real and worthwhile. They discussed horses and the differences in the way English and American people rode them. All the while Carrie felt so relaxed and content that she quietly wished they could stay all night.

Sally and Stephen seemed to have found some more stories about celebrities that amused them so Caleb and Carrie just enjoyed swapping stories about their lives. Carrie did not remember feeling this relaxed with anyone new since she met Matt and was trying hard not to think about that. She was trying not to notice how attentive and how HOT Caleb was! Not only was he out of her league, he lived in

America and she was NOT looking for either a partner or a quick thrill. She knew he was just being a gentleman and acting interested in her dull little life. The thrill she felt when he handed her her drink and their fingers touched was just the result of her celibate lifestyle she told herself. As if he was interested in her anyway, she bet he could have the pick of hundreds of women. Why was she even thinking like this? It was time to go home. She had really enjoyed the evening but it was just what it was, an evening out in good company, no more.

Carrie caught Sally's attention and looked at her watch. If they were going to manage a 6am start they needed to get home soon as it was nearly midnight with an hours journey ahead. Caleb saw her and immediately took charge. He called for his car as they finished their drinks. A couple of rings on Caleb's phone signalled the car's arrival and they headed outside. All four piled into the large and luxurious car and the journey to Elver began.

Sally was enthralled with the car, it was a Tesla apparently and very swish. It was Sally and Carrie's first ride in an electric car and they were impressed. "Will it have enough charge to get us home and you back safely?" Sally asked. Caleb laughed and Stephen went off into a detailed explanation about the new technology. Neither woman was really following the lecture but it seemed they needn't worry about anyone getting stranded! Caleb sat between Carrie and Sally in the back of the roomy car and he grinned and winked at Carrie as Stephen droned on. He had obviously heard it all before. Sally appeared to be asleep as they reached the M11 and Stephen was quiet in the front. Caleb gently whispered to Carrie, "Thanks for a lovely evening, I'm so glad we bumped into you both."

Carrie replied, "We should be thanking you for the meal and the ride home, I hope you don't have to work tomorrow?"

Caleb shook his head,"I have a couple of meetings but they're not early. It's you two that have an early start."

Caleb was quiet for a moment then he gently put his hand on Carrie's and whispered, "I haven't told anyone else this because they wouldn't understand, but I am done with Hollywood society. I've been fantasizing about making changes for years but never had the guts to break away. I have a dream of running a sanctuary for unwanted and neglected animals one day. It'll be a while away yet, but after tonight I feel empowered – you and Sally have reminded me just how false my life has been all these years. I love acting, and will never give that up, but the whole celebrity lifestyle thing is just so not me any more. Thank you for giving me a glimpse into a real life tonight. I feel I have been given an insight and I intend to change things going forward."

Carrie was shocked that Caleb had shared this with her, and didn't really know what to say. She turned her hand in his and squeezed his fingers. "I wish you all the luck in the world Caleb, and it's been such a lovely evening. I'll treasure the memory of meeting you. Thank you for rescuing me earlier when I had a wobble – you made me feel safe whilst I got myself together. Grief never really goes away, it seems to hit hardest just when you think you've got a handle on it. I look forward to reading about the changes in your life – it might make reading Sally's awful gossip magazines bearable!" Caleb laughed so loud that Sally woke with a start, but she soon dropped off again.

Half an hour later they were approaching Elver and home. Carrie suddenly realised she had been sitting there for all this time with her hand still lightly holding Caleb's. She pulled away gently and busied herself in her handbag so as not to catch his eye. Sally awoke just as they pulled into the stable yard. She and Carrie got out of the car and Caleb jumped out to give them a big hug. Stephen was fast asleep in the front seat of the Tesla so Carrie asked Caleb to pass on her phone number to him. She fumbled in her bag for a pen. "My mobile's broken and I haven't managed to get a new one yet, this is my house phone number," she said, handing a scrap of paper to Caleb. "If you can pass it to Stephen, I would love for Ellie to call me for a catch up sometime."

Caleb looked surprised. "I've never met someone who could be calm about not having a mobile phone," he laughed. "If mine broke I'd have a new one within 10 minutes!"

"That's the downside of living in the real world," said Carrie smiling. "My budget won't stretch to a new phone for a few more weeks so I have to manage till then. After our conversation earlier – just be careful what you wish for!" She winked and he gave her a huge grin as he got back in the car.

Carrie and Sally waved as the car pulled away then snuck quietly into Sally's house. Carrie was staying in the guest room, as she had a few times before when a late night or early morning made it easier. The friends giggled as they crept up the stairs and into their rooms. "We'll chat in the morning Carrie but that was an amazing night," said Sally.

"It was, sleep tight," said Carrie, as she shut her bedroom door and let out a sigh. She was exhausted but had a feeling sleep would take a while. She found herself giggling at her reflection as she cleaned her teeth, and nearly choked on the toothpaste! "OK time for bed you idiot!" she told herself, grinning into the mirror.

Night Matt – miss you.

Chapter 4

After glow

Carrie woke with a start as she heard a knock on her door. Sally's head appeared, damn if her hair didn't look good even at six in the morning. "Kettle's on and it's time to face reality," she grinned. Carrie stretched and forced herself to wake fully. After a quick shower and finding her work clothes she shuffled downstairs to face the day. A cup of tea and some toast cleared her head. Sally was bounding downstairs ready to go by the time she had cleared up. They didn't say much to each other until the horses were all turned out in the fields and the stables were peacefully empty – just needing a good muck out. As they gathered the forks, brooms and wheelbarrows they finally had time to chat about their night.

"Oh my God Carrie, what a night," said Sally, as she started on the first stable. "Let's do each stable together so we can chat, I'm still on cloud nine!" Usually, they did half the yard each, for speed, but Sally was the boss – and Carrie wanted to chat too.

"You only saw two of your celebrities, was that

enough to hold you for a while?" grinned Carrie.

"Oh I think so!" laughed Sally. "Caleb Kirk-michael is equal to twenty EastEnders actors, and he hugged me, and he paid for my dinner, and he brought us home, and he was soooo hot! That should keep me happy for months, in fact, I'm not sure how I can top that, the next trip will be a total anticlimax!"

Carrie was laughing so hard that Sally looked a bit abashed, "What's so funny?"

"I don't think you breathed once during that sentence Sally!" said Carrie. "And your face lit up like a little kid at Christmas."

"I'm just so hyped, I can't wait to read more about him and find out all his dirty secrets," said Sally happily. Carrie flinched inwardly at that thought, Caleb had seemed so nice she didn't want to think about him having any scandal written about him, that would spoil the illusion. She shook herself – as if it would matter anyway – the Caleb she talked to was probably just an act, no more real than the tabloid version. She would hold onto the memory and disassociate him from the film star in the news. He could be her private fantasy, the thought made her feel like a teenager and she grinned to herself.

Sally was watching Carrie now, looking a little deeper at her friend. "Do I get the feeling you and

Caleb made a bit of a connection last night Carrie?"

Carrie studied a bit of horse muck far more thoroughly than necessary, while she thought how to answer Sally's question. "I don't think it was a two-way thing," she said slowly. "I was blown away by his kindness, and the fact he was so normal was a surprise, but he's an actor, he was probably just playing the part. I felt more positive emotion last night than I've felt since Matt, but that was all. I don't think it was more than a fun evening. Anyway, what are the chances of ever seeing someone like that again? I'll look on it as a sign that my life is finally moving forward. I felt the hots for two cute guys, met with an old friend and almost managed a whole evening without blubbing, all good things I guess."

Sally, sensing a change of topic was needed, replied, "Ooh who was the other cute guy?"

"Just a very hunky waiter, and before you ask, no future there either as I might have shouted at him a teensie bit. Well, I hope I was assertive and constructive, but I was a bit angry!" They laughed as they worked, both getting lost in their own thoughts.

By lunchtime, most of the hard work was finished and the stables stood ready for their occupants to be in overnight. Hay-nets and water buckets were filled and the muck heap was tidy. An afternoon of exercising a few horses before bringing the others in from the fields stretched ahead. The best part of the day. As the women came out of the house after lunch a courier van pulled in at the gate. Sally rushed over to take the delivery. When she came back she was carrying two huge bunches of flowers and a box.

"Wow!" said Carrie, "late Birthday gifts?"

"I don't think so," smiled Sally, "two of them have your name on."

Sally handed a bunch of flowers and the box to Carrie and ripped the card from her own bunch. "They're from Caleb!" Sally squealed as she read the card. "He says thanks for a lovely evening and he wished he could have introduced me to more celebrities so I could have got my fix. Aww, that's so sweet, and I have his autograph now too. I must go in and show Terry."

Carrie laughed, "Will Terry mind you getting flowers from another man?"

Sally's smile dimmed for a second then she said, "Nah, he'll be fine," and ran inside.

Carrie looked down at her bunch of flowers, they were really stunning. She couldn't remember the last time she had flowers. She thought of Matt and teared up just a little. She opened the card and read.

Hi Carrie

*I hope you like the flowers and the other gift.
We had such a great time last night, I am still
grinning as I write this.*

*I have started with my grand plan to leave
Hollywood this morning by putting my big
house there on the market. I am not sure where
I will choose to live next but it will be
somewhere I can be me, Caleb, and not Mr
Kirkmichael or Sir.*

*I will have land around me, horses grazing and
no sycophantic lackeys around at all – in my
dreams at least.*

*How I can balance that with carrying on as an
actor I'm not sure yet – but I will.*

Wish me luck,

With Love

Caleb xxx

She hugged the note to her for a second and
wished him luck, then carefully stashed it away in
her pocket. Looking down at the box she wondered
what else Caleb could have sent, maybe some
scrummy chocolates? She tore off the wrapping

almost salivating at the thought. Then she stopped and drew a breath. The name on the box was not Milk Tray or Roses – it was Samsung! Maybe the chocolates were inside for protection? She opened the box and saw a shiny new phone staring back at her. "Oh my goodness, what do I do now?" she said out loud. She really didn't think she should accept such a generous gift. There was another note tucked inside the see-through bag the phone was in. She saw her name on the front. Carrie withdrew the note from the bag, unfolded it and read.

Dear Carrie

I was walking through the temporary office I have here in London and I saw this box sitting on a shelf. I realised that part of the life I lead is about excess – and it's not a part I really like any more. We bought 12 phones for all my staff here in the UK whilst I am filming. They are all on one contract with unlimited hours, roaming and data, each has its own number and the contract is for at least a year, depending on where I am filming next year. We only actually bought 9 staff with us and I have the 10th. The 11th was faulty but no one has bothered to do anything about it. I am so stupidly rich because of some success in my chosen career and I hate what it has made me become. I have become so wasteful and selfish that a perfectly good phone was sat there *unused, whilst someone like you 'in the real world' struggles on without one. I hate to think of you out riding or out alone at night without a phone for emergencies.*

Please please accept this phone and use it however you want. If you keep the sim that's in it you will not have any phone bills for at least a year, but you can put your own sim in if you want. I have saved my own private number in the contacts – you never know when you might fancy a chat?

Please don't think badly of me and my excess – I am finally seeing the light.

Love

Caleb xxx

By the time she had read the second note she was in tears and Sally came rushing over to hug her. "Whatever did your note say? Was he unkind? I'll kill him!!"

Carrie just handed it to her and scrabbled for a tissue. After Sally read the note, twice, she was tearing up as well. "What do I do Sally, should I keep it?"

"Keep the phone and ring him you daft mare, he's

too good to miss!" said Sally. Carrie smiled and put the phone in her pocket. It would be a nice reminder of her fantasy man, not that she would dare to ring him but a text now and then might be possible – just to be polite.

Imagine that Matt!

Chapter 5

Breaking Moulds

The flowers were beautiful and lasted nearly two weeks before they had to be thrown out. Carrie definitely threw them all out and absolutely did not press and dry one to keep in her purse! She had texted Caleb with a 'Thank You' for the flowers and phone but had not heard anything from him since. Life was back in a routine and she guessed that was where it should be. The weather was getting hotter by the day and she was coming home exhausted from work. All the horses were out in the fields 24/7 now so the mucking out was history, but haymaking and a million other jobs kept them busy. By the evening she was happy to get a cool drink and just sit chatting to her housemates or chilling in her own little sitting room.

Dave and Gregg had made her tell the story of their amazing evening so many times over the last two weeks. They were big fans of Caleb Kirkmichael films and were quite graphic about how hot he was! They asked every night if she had heard from him and could not understand why she didn't call him. "They're filming a big Wartime movie in Kent apparently so I expect he's very busy," Dave told her one evening. "One of my old workmates is building some sets for a big county house they are using, so he said in the pub last week." Carrie kind of wished they would stop talking about him – she didn't need any help remembering. She hoped if she kept quiet they would soon lose interest in matchmaking, it was a lost cause anyway. Carrie loved her housemates, but their determination to find her a fairytale ending was just that – a fairytale.

*   *   *   *   *

One evening Carrie answered the landline at home and heard a familiar voice – it was Stephen's wife and her old friend Ellie.

"Carrie, how are you? It's been so long since we spoke. Stephen was very excited to have seen you the other week."

"Ellie bee, thank you for ringing. It was so surreal seeing Stephen like that. We had a great time catching up. I hear you have two little ones now?"

"Yes, Poppy and Christopher, they are my world these days. I'm a stay at home Mum, but I still manage to write between the School runs and clubs. I freelance now for a couple of companies that publish scientific books. I hear you met Caleb that night too, he's a sweetie, always bringing presents for the kids, Stephen loves working with

him. The film industry is a strange world and Stephen struggled to make connections but Caleb always asks for him to do his special effects, he's really helped Stephen get a good name."

"I'm not surprised, Caleb seemed such a nice person. Did Stephen tell you I was widowed? It's been a couple of years and I think I am getting my life together a bit better these days. I gave up my career and I work with horses now, the pay is terrible but I love it."

"Yes he did and I am so sorry. I remember Matt, such a shame. By the way, Stephen says hi. He also says Caleb mentions you a bit. I think he found you refreshing company, maybe we could set up a dinner party and invite Caleb and you?"

"Listen, Ellie, I would love to talk more but I have to go out in a minute. We must catch up again soon. It's been too long.........bye."

Carrie hung up hurriedly and let out a sigh. When would people stop trying to be a matchmaker for her! Didn't they understand, Matt died, he didn't just leave, how could she go on as if nothing happened?

* * * * *

It was a few days later, and she knew the lads had planned themselves a good night out. She was looking forward to an evening of peace and solitude. She'd have a good long shower, then sit watching TV or reading. She had scraped together enough spare change for fish and chips, so no cooking or washing up to do. As she let herself into the house with her meal under her arm she really looked forward to some quiet time. She ate her meal in the downstairs lounge watching the news. She was still in her dirty work clothes but no one was there to be offended so she couldn't be bothered to change. As the news wound up there was the usual light story at the end. Her eyes lit up when a shot of Caleb appeared. The story was about an award ceremony that was happening that night in London. The still shots were of the stars arriving and going down the red carpet.

As she watched the coverage went live. Watching faces that she didn't know, in dresses and suits that probably cost more than she would earn in six months, she wondered how Caleb was feeling. Would he be dreading the evening or would he lap up the attention? As she watched he appeared, looking totally at ease in a very sharp suit, with a young lady on his arm. She tried not to look at her. The cameras swarmed and there was a volley of flashes going off. The reporter for the News stuck a mike under his nose and asked how filming was going on the new project. Caleb gave some slick and polite answer that told her nothing and smiled at the cameras. Carrie tried not to feel anything, but her heart flipped at that smile. By the time she started concentrating again, the reporter was wrapping up and saying the ceremony was being televised on their sister channel tonight. Well, at least she knew what she would be watching!

After a quick shower and change, Carrie sat on her bed with her tiny TV playing the music for the start of the Awards. She had no idea if Caleb had won anything but she hoped she would, at least, get a glimpse of him again. She asked herself why she was watching something that had her in turmoil but knew she would watch it anyway. Once the ceremony got going she realised it could be a long wait to see him, too many people with too much to say about themselves. She was almost dozing off after half an hour when the camera did a sweep of the audience, and there he was, looking bored and fed up, at least until he spotted the camera on him! Then the smile took over. She laughed, what a world to live in. As the camera moved on she found herself picking up her phone. Dare she text him now and see if he responded? Before she could chicken out she bought up his number and dashed off a quick text.

Hi Caleb, you look bored, how's the new life coming on? C xx

She pressed send and kept watching hoping she would see him again. For a few minutes, all was quiet then her phone pinged, almost stopping her heart. She picked up the phone hardly daring to hope.

Hi Carrie, So good to hear from you. Are you watching this at home? It is soooo boring. The more time I spend at these things the more I wish I could muck out horses for a living, you have the right idea I think. C xx

She smiled, wondering if he had ever experienced what living without money was like.

Hi Caleb. Yes I am. I can find you a stable to muck out any time you want to practice ;-)

Hi C, I should be going on stage in about half an hour to collect something – you can tell me if I sound as boring and self loving as the others, LOL. I will wave at you when I'm up there! C xx

Oooh, what did you win? Xx

You will see in half an hour if you can bear to watch that long! Xx

I'll be watching, unlikely to get a better offer tonight, LOL. Xx

I don't know whether to be flattered or not by that? ;-) speak soon. Xx

Carrie was shaking by the time the little volley of texts had finished, shaking and grinning. She quickly went down for a cup of tea whilst the adverts were on then plonked herself down to watch and wait.

The presenter announces:

> **"And the Winner of Best Male Lead is .... Caleb Kirkmichael for his performance in The Wind World."**

Loud cheering from his table as he gets up and approaches the stage, kissing the odd beautiful lady as he passes.

He mounts the steps and stands at the mike.

He waves and winks at the camera.

"OMG was that for me?" said Carrie.

And says some stuff about a film blah blah blah.

And then he holds up the statue thingy and says;

"Here's to the beginning of a new life, thank you Carrie."

And the crowd goes wild.

And Carrie pinches herself and laughs like a madwoman.

The adverts start again while Carrie just stares and giggles.

"OMG – did that actually happen?" Carrie asked herself out loud. She fumbled for her phone and typed out a quick text.

I can't believe you just did that, you are going to get so many questions now! C Xx

There was no proper answer from Caleb, just a smile emoji and C *Xxxxx.* Carrie settled back on her bed and picked up her book, knowing she would not read a word.

What just happened Matt?

Chapter 6

Analysis

Dave and Gregg came home around 11pm and found Carrie asleep on the downstairs couch in her dressing gown. She woke as the kettle went on in the kitchen. "How do you do that?" laughed Gregg. "I assume you would like a cup?" Carrie nodded then remembered why she had waited up for them.

"Dave, can you show me how to find something on catch up? There was an awards ceremony on channel 2 earlier and I want to watch it again." Dave looked surprised, then nodded knowingly.

"Was lover boy getting a gong?" he asked.

"Something like that," she agreed grumpily.

"I'll have a look for you but not everything will be available so don't hold your breath." Carrie went into the kitchen to help with the tea while Dave searched for the programme on their big TV in the lounge. When she and Gregg returned he was watching the ceremony.

"How far in was his bit?" asked Dave.

"About an hour in," said Carrie.

He fast-forwarded about an hour and stopped it just as Caleb mounted the stage. They all watched as he winked and waved at the camera. "That was a strange thing to do," Dave muttered, but Carrie just smiled. His speech went on for a couple of minutes and then the bit that was etched on her brain came up. Dave and Gregg just gasped and looked at her. "What new life, and is he talking to you?" asked Gregg.

"Do we need to buy new dresses and hats love?" asked Dave, grinning at her.

"No," she said, "it's nothing like that."

"Aww and I so wanted a new dress, what's going on then?" asked Gregg.

"I'm not totally sure myself," admitted Carrie, "and I know it doesn't involve me, except he said that I'd inspired him to make changes in his life. I'm sure it'll be headline news if he does anything out of the ordinary. Night guys and thanks for the tea."

*   *   *   *   *

Carrie was at work before 6am the next morning,

sleep had been elusive, she needed to be busy. She had the early jobs done before Sally appeared. "No need to ask if you watched the Awards last night?" Sally joked as she arrived in the tack room with two mugs of tea.

"What do you mean?" asked Carrie.

"Whenever something is bothering you, you're here getting our jobs done before I wake up."

Of course, Sally would have watched the Awards Ceremony last night, thought Carrie, all those celebs in one place and dolled up to the nines. "Oh Sally, I am so confused by my feelings. I know Caleb is not ever going to be interested in me and I know I don't want a relationship or even a quick fling. Why am I still thinking about him so much that I can't sleep?"

Sally smiled. "Maybe because you haven't allowed anyone through your defences in almost three years, maybe because he's as cute as a puppy, maybe because he seems to want to get to know you, maybe because you do actually want to love again, if you could let yourself? Is that enough reasons?"

"I hate you – you know that don't you?" laughed Carrie. "You are so bloody wise!" They giggled and got on with their day.

Carrie was towing a horse muck sweeper around

the far paddocks with Sally's little tractor when thoughts of what Sally said started to invade her calm. Muck clearing didn't take much brainpower and her mind was wandering. Was Sally right, was it possible that she could love someone apart from Matt? Was that what this was about? Obviously, she could never be in a relationship with Caleb – he was just unobtainable, but maybe the darker recesses of her heart were telling her to be open to possibilities? Maybe it was her defences that chose Caleb to kick start her feelings because he was safe, he was so out of her league. Oh god – this was too deep. She just needed to forget Caleb and let life carry her along for a bit. Concentrate on driving in a straight line woman, she thought – forget 'that meal' or you will still be muck clearing at midnight.

I am working this out Matt.

Chapter 7

Horse Talk

For the next few weeks, Carrie's life was extremely normal. Work was busy, with getting summer jobs done while the horses were out in the fields. Riding still took up most of their afternoons and by the time Carrie got home each evening she was ready to relax with the lads or with a good book. She had even managed to keep her thoughts under control – most of the time. Thoughts of 'that meal' were consciously pushed out of her head if they snuck in. She didn't hear from Caleb and did not let herself text him – it was just a fun evening!

Strangely, thoughts of Matt were becoming more common, but she found that she could think of him without the sadness she had had for years. She was allowing herself to remember all the great times they shared, and finally, she could remember him, the real him, without falling apart. Weirdly she realised her grief had stolen him from her far more than his physical loss. Now she could remember him with a smile, she felt closer to him than she had for years. As her family were long gone and his had moved away after "that time" she had never really had anyone to reminisce with about her marriage. She only met Sally and the lads after Matt was gone. The few other friends she and Matt had, drifted away when her grief was too much to bear. She suddenly realised how alone she had been and was a little bit proud that she had survived. Now it was time to stop surviving and start living again, Matt would approve she was sure. She suddenly remembered his amazing smile and smiled right back at him – she felt him so strongly and she knew she was heading for brighter times.

Carrie decided to share her new feelings with Sally over a long tack cleaning session one wet afternoon. Riding was cancelled as Sally felt the fields were too slippery and the riding arena was being resurfaced. To be honest the sudden rain made both of them happy to stay indoors so it wasn't a hard decision.

She described to Sally how she could think about Matt without breaking down. She explained how being able to think of him made her feel she had that part of her life, and part of him, back at last. Sally gave her a big, saddle soapy hug and they stopped for another brew to celebrate.

*   *   *   *   *

Carrie arrived at work a few days later and she could feel Sally was itching to tell her something. As soon as they had done the morning checks of the horses in the fields Sally said, "Let's have a cuppa, there's something I need to talk to you about, I'm soooo excited." They sat, with their tea, on a couple of hay bales and Sally said, "I had a phone call last night asking me if I could do a riding lesson for two adults who need to brush up their skills."

"That's strange. Do they think we are a riding school, did you give them the number of the one in Bunton?"

"Ummm, not exactly. I said I would do it. I had to check my insurance but I am covered. I can use Sadie and borrow Nero, his owners owe me a favour. The thing is........the people I will be teaching are Caleb Kirkmichael and Simon Clinton! It will be lovely to see Caleb again but I so want to meet Simon Clinton, he was in that US lawyer drama that I raved about last year, do you remember?"

"No, not really, but I've heard of him. Why on earth do they want a riding lesson? Is it for a film or something? I'm sure Caleb said he could ride. Why here, don't the film studios have people they use for all that?"

"Slow down Carrie," laughed Sally. "They're both, apparently, in the same film, which they're making in the US a bit later in the year. Although it's an American film they need to ride convincingly like we do, English style, not western. Caleb says he's ridden English style before but needs a refresher. Apparently, Simon had only ever ridden once and fell off. Luckily he has simple riding to do, walking mainly, but Caleb thinks he may have some cantering for his part."

"OK, that makes sense, but why here?"

"That's the amusing part, they both went to have a lesson with the person their UK agent booked and apparently she was an old dragon! A real, old school horsewoman who shouted at them the whole time and pushed Simon well beyond his ability and confidence. Now he is refusing to even get on a horse."

"Oh, poor chap. I remember a riding instructor like that, she nearly put me off riding too!"

Sally continued, "Caleb wants to help Simon get over his fear but there's no way they are going back to the old dragon. Caleb found out she has been used by film companies for years and the UK agent wasn't very helpful when asked if they could try someone else. He remembered we have horses and asked me if they could come here, in secret, and practice enough to get Simon confident again. He thought we'd have more patience, and I suspect he knew I wouldn't be able to say no to meeting another celebrity!"

"So when are they coming?" asked Carrie.

"Tomorrow afternoon. Are you OK seeing Caleb again? I know he stirred up a few emotions last time."

Carrie thought about it. "I think I'm more realistic about things now. I'm sure I'll be fine, and he was so nice, it'll be lovely to see him again."

"Thank goodness!" said Sally. "I so want to meet Simon Clinton but I was worried you'd be upset by Caleb being here. I'd say take the afternoon off but I think I'll need you to lead Sadie so Simon feels safe."

"Maybe if I lead Simon around the outside of the arena, while you teach Caleb inside, he will build up enough confidence to do more by the time Caleb is finished?"

"That's a great idea," said Sally, "we'll try that. I wonder how much riding Caleb's done?"

"We'll find out tomorrow. 'Sally Walker, Riding instructor to the Stars!' It has a good ring to it," laughed Carrie.

*   *   *   *   *

At 2pm the following afternoon the big Tesla pulled onto the yard. No one would know who was in the back, the windows seemed to be mirror glass or something. Carrie thought it was very movie star looking, she hadn't noticed the windows last time, but it was dark then. The driver parked up and the two men got out. Carrie's heart did a major flip when she saw Caleb in jodhpurs and long riding boots. Wow! She studied Simon Clinton instead – much safer for her emotions. Sally had rushed to greet them so Carrie busied herself getting the horses ready, despite the fact that they had already finished that ten minutes ago. Simon looked familiar to Carrie but she could not think what she'd seen him in. He was tall and handsome, in a clean and 'town living' sort of way. He didn't have that 'rough edged' look that Caleb had. She couldn't imagine him shirtless and dirty in an action movie, but she bet he played a good lawyer.

They were heading towards her now so she smiled and moved to greet them. Caleb stepped close and gave her a hug, shaking her calmness a little. "How have you been Carrie? Good to see you again."

"Hi Caleb, I'm good, how are you?"

"I'm good too. Thanks for brightening up my evening at the Award Ceremony, by the way, I really enjoyed your texts. Sorry I went quiet after a while. I got nabbed by the Film Company CEO and he talked for hours. I've been so busy filming here and preparing for the next film in the US. I love being busy but I do tend to get totally preoccupied with work. It's wonderful to have a trip out of London to enjoy some fresh air, and some good company of course!" he said winking.

Carrie turned to Simon, "It's lovely to meet you, Mr Clinton." She shook his hand.

"Call me Simon," he smiled. "You'll probably see me crying like a baby in a few minutes, so let's not stand on ceremony." They all laughed at that.

Sally introduced them to the horses and checked their riding hats and footwear were suitable. "I think we'll get Simon on first, don't panic Simon, we'll all be there to support you, and there's no rush. Let's get Sadie out of her stable then you can spend a few moments getting to know her." Carrie led Sadie out and stood her in front of Simon. "Just run your hands over her neck, give her a pat, let her sniff your hand, make friends." He did, hesitantly. "Carrie, show Simon how to hold her head and he can lead her to the mounting block."

Carrie showed him how to hold the reins just behind Sadie's mouth and said, "Simon, use the words 'Walk On' in a firm but gentle voice and just walk forward – she will come with you." Sadie happily walked beside Simon as they headed to the block. "Well done Simon," smiled Sally. "Now gently pull on the reins and say 'Stand', whilst stopping yourself."

"She understands me," Simon said with glee. "I speak horse!"

Carrie took the reins from Simon and positioned Sadie next to the mounting block, which was really just a small platform with steps at one end. "OK Simon," said Sally, "come with me and we'll get you on the block and show you how to get on Sadie safely." Simon mounted the steps and stood beside Sadie. He looked worried so Sally said, "Just stand there for a minute, give her a pat again and catch your breath."

"I can feel my stress levels rising, I'm not sure I can do this," Simon said. He was shaking. Sally could feel it through the block.

"Just stand and breathe, there's no hurry."

Simon touched Sadie's neck and stroked her. He did some deep breathing and swallowed hard. "OK next step."

Sally stood behind him on the block and held his hips. "Sorry to be so intimate but I can support you while you mount, so you feel secure, and hell no, I'm not sorry at all!" giggled Sally.

"I like your style," laughed Simon, relaxing visibly.

Sally watched as he put his foot into the stirrup. She reminded him to take a breath and he shakily put his weight into the stirrup and swung his other leg over, sitting down onto the saddle. Sadie stood like a rock and everyone else breathed a sigh. "Well done Simon, that's the hardest bit done. Now I suggest you just stand there for a bit, Carrie will be holding Sadie, just let yourself relax. Carrie, once Simon is ready, can you walk him very slowly around the outside of the arena. Caleb, come with me and we'll get you mounted on Nero and you can ride in the arena."

Caleb and Sally headed off and Carrie chatted with Simon whilst he tried to relax. "How are you feeling Simon?" Carrie asked.

"A bit better now, can we stay here for a bit?"

"Of course we can, why don't you try leaning forward a little bit and stroking her neck. That's it, well done. Now gently twist from your waist and touch her back, behind the saddle, well done Simon. Let's get really brave now, put both hands on your knees, good, now slide your hands down your legs and see if you can touch your feet. Bend from the waist, just go as far as you feel OK with. My what long legs you have!"

Simon giggled as he bent down towards his feet. Carrie knew laughter would make him relax. "How did that feel?" she asked.

"Weird but OK. I feel much more relaxed now."

"Shall we try a gentle walk round?"

"Yes please."

Carrie checked he had hold of the reins loosely and told him to use the words 'Walk On' again. She was leading Sadie so he didn't have anything to do except sit still. They walked around the track for a few minutes whilst Caleb was riding around inside the arena. "How are the stress levels now Simon?"

"Not bad Carrie, Sadie's walk is like a gentle rocking, it's soothing. The horse I was on at the other place felt a bit more bumpy, I felt like I might fall off."

Carrie smiled to herself. "Was it more like this?" she said, asking Sadie to walk faster.

"Yes sort of, only worse," said Simon, tensing up.

Carrie slowed Sadie again, "That's just a faster walk, nothing to fear. Just think of it as the difference between strolling along and power walking."

"That helps, I can understand that analogy, thanks."

"Shall we try some steering?" Carrie went on to explain how to steer Sadie and how to stop her. They practised for a while and having something to concentrate on helped Simon relax more. After a while, he was confident enough to watch Caleb riding around as they walked. Caleb was cantering around the arena and looking like a natural rider, as he passed them he winked at her.

"When can I try a trot Carrie?" Simon asked.

She laughed. "This, from the man who was never getting on a horse again 20 minutes ago? When Sally and Caleb have finished we can go into the arena and try a trot. For now, let's see if you can steer and stop without me leading you."

By the time Caleb and Sally had finished Simon was riding without being led, was getting Sadie to go wherever he asked and stop and go on command. Caleb dismounted and took Nero back to his stable. Carrie took Simon into the school and went to check on Caleb, while Sally watched what Simon could do at a walk.

As she neared Nero's stable she could hear Caleb chatting to the horse. She stopped to listen, not wanting to spoil the moment. "Well that was fun lad, thank you, it must be like riding a bike, you never forget. I think I might ache a bit in the morning though. Maybe in my heart as well as my muscles, what a hopeless case I am, hey old boy? Maybe it will happen one day?" Carrie did not know what that was about but she could feel his compassion for Nero and she was impressed. He was obviously an animal lover, maybe he would get his Animal Shelter one day. She coughed loudly so Caleb knew she was coming and entered the stable to help him untack. Once Nero was comfortably eating hay and the tack was put away Carrie and Caleb headed back to the arena.

Simon was trotting around the arena, without help, and was grinning. "Wow Sally," said Caleb. "You've done a great job."

Sally smiled and said, "I think we have Carrie to thank, she had Simon so relaxed by the time he came in here that trotting was no bother. Well done Carrie."

Carrie looked embarrassed and said, "Simon was great, he's the star! And I think seeing Caleb cantering around may have brought out a teensie bit of competitive spirit too. Typical bloke!"

Sally told Simon to walk round a couple of times to wind down and then helped him dismount. "I feel like I can cope with anything now. Thank you ladies," Simon said. He reached for Carrie and gave her a big hug and a kiss on the cheek. As he moved away to hug Sally, Carrie caught Caleb's expression, just for a second he looked.......what? Almost angry? But then it was gone. She went and stood next to Caleb and touched his arm. "Do you feel ready for your filming now?"

"Yes I think I do, I felt pleased with how quickly the English style of riding came back to me. Sally seemed happy with me anyway, and Nero is a lovely chap, shame he won't fit in the Tesla or I'd take him with me," he replied. Carrie giggled. He put his arm around her in a friendly manner and said, "Thanks Carrie, for helping Simon, I watched you while I was riding round and you really took care of him." He gently squeezed her and kissed the top of her head.

Suddenly Simon cursed and said, "Caleb, look at the time, I have to be back in town by 5.30, we must fly." Simon hastily handed Sally the money for the lessons, full of thanks, Caleb squeezed Carrie again, thanked Sally and they jogged to the car and left.

"Wow, what an afternoon, he was dreamy," sighed Sally.

"Did you get an autograph?" asked Carrie.

"Bugger," said Sally.

After that unique afternoon, Carrie felt a little flat as she walked home. To see Caleb a second time had been wonderful but now she needed to accept that it was all over. He was just a couple of exciting moments in her dull life, not part of her future. If she wanted a new and fulfilling life she needed to get real about Caleb and put him out of her mind. She would never move forward if she didn't. She made a pact with herself – no more fantasy man. No more dreaming.

I need a real future, not a fairytale one Matt.

Chapter 8

Fame

On Sunday, just over a week after the riding lesson, Sally was in the newsagents stocking up on her gossipy show biz magazines. She looked at the selection on the shelf and sighed, so much choice these days and so many grubby stories. Maybe it was time to grow out of this addiction of hers and just buy the Horse and Hound like any normal horse-lover. She laughed at the idea and grabbed a handful of her favourite mags, with a horse magazine on top, for appearances.

When Sally got home she decided she had plenty of time to spare for a cup of coffee and a quick flick through her purchases. She had a routine of flicking through the magazines, noting the really good gossip and then reading each one in turn for the details. She was about three magazines into her pile when she flicked passed a photo with a very familiar feel. She took a closer look and saw it was a photo of Simon Clinton with a girl in his arms. The photo was cropped close, clearly showing his face. She looked closer and realised the 'girl' was her – she'd recognise that scruffy old shirt anywhere, what the........! At least she had her back to the camera and her face was hidden. The next shot was of Carrie, arm in arm with Caleb. Both Caleb and Carrie were clearly recognisable in this one. The shot showed more background - it was obviously her riding arena. The final shot was a grainy close up of Caleb hugging Carrie with his lips pressed to the top of her head! OMG – they'd been papped! How did the photographer know the men were here, for God's sake? Sally felt a sense of horror. Had she let slip to anyone? How did the photographer get in without anyone seeing? She studied the picture with more background, the photographer must have pushed himself right through the tall thick hedge along the roadside to get a clear shot – she hoped the brambles tore him to shreds, Bastard! She hurriedly read the headline.

Have we found Carrie?

Caleb Kirkmichael kisses mystery woman.

And who is the latest woman in Simon Clinton's arms?

She read the smaller text, there was a rehash of Caleb's comments at the awards ceremony and more speculation about if he was retiring from public life.

There was nothing about where the pictures were taken, thank goodness. The article did say that 'local sources' confirmed the woman in Caleb's arms was called Carrie though, oh shit.

Sally thought she should warn Caleb. She had his number from when he booked the riding lesson so she phoned him straight away. As soon as he answered the phone he said:

"Sally, yes I've seen it, the publicity department for the new film is over the moon! Bloody scum of the earth, sneaky bastard journalists, how did Carrie take it? Is she OK?"

"I haven't spoken to her yet I rang you first. I will ring her in a sec. How did they find you here?"

"I've just spoken with Simon. He says he has been hounded by this lot for weeks, they have been following him around. He thinks someone on his team is tipping them off whenever he goes out somewhere. He did not think to mention it before we led them to you and Carrie! I'm so sorry Sally, they must have followed the car from London."

"No harm done to me – you can't recognise me in the picture and they haven't mentioned the location, thank God. Unfortunately, Carrie is clearly recognisable and they confirm her first name, she may get some stick locally."

"I know. I feel so bad for her, and you, I should have known better than to mix you both up in our sordid world. This is the part of being in films that I want to distance myself from, and now I've just managed to bring it to your door." Caleb sounded almost tearful.

"Caleb, it's OK, we will all survive, I will talk to Carrie and show her the article. She may be a little upset at first but I'm sure she will see the funny side, eventually. I am never buying another one of these magazines though – it is horrible to be on the receiving end of what I thought of as harmless cheap journalism. I feel dirty now," she laughed.

"Should I ring her too, Sally, will she want to talk to me?"

"I don't know Caleb, let me talk to her first."

"OK Sally, can you tell her how sorry I am, and give her a hug for me please?"

Sally laughed, "Hugs are what got us into this mess! Bye Caleb."

She ended the call and sat back to think. After a while, she picked up the offending magazine and headed out to see Carrie.

Luckily everyone was at home when Sally arrived. Dave opened the door and welcomed her in. She quickly showed him the article and said, "I need to talk to Carrie about this and warn her, can you be here too, in case she is really upset?"

Dave scanned through the photos and text and whistled "Oh dear Lord, she will not be happy, it is obvious it's her. Damn, she seems so much stronger at the minute, I hope this doesn't set her back too much. I'll call her down, and Gregg, he's good in a crisis."

Soon Carrie and Gregg appeared and Sally began. "Carrie I have something to show you and you're not going to like it. Gregg, you might want to read it over her shoulder?"

Carrie took the magazine and stared at the photos. "How?" was all she said at first. She read the text and giggled, "What a load of horse shit, why would anyone be interested in who I am anyway. I'm glad no one mentioned you or the yard Sally, that could have been bad for business. At least your face is hidden so no harm done."

She read it again and looked at the pictures in detail. "Well, you don't need Simon's autograph now Sally – you have a sexy picture instead! I look ridiculously short next to Caleb, does my bum look big?" Suddenly she gasped, "Poor Caleb, I wonder if he's seen them, he will be embarrassed to be linked romantically with someone like me."

Sally looked surprised. "Caleb has seen it, I rang him as soon as I found it and he already knew. He was so worried that you would be upset and very angry with the magazine. He said I was to apologise on his behalf and to give you a hug from him." Sally put her arms around Carrie and they hugged. "Are you worried that local people will recognise you Carrie?"

"I was just beginning to think of that, but who do I know? If neighbours happen to read this stuff then they might see me in a different light I guess, but so what? Oh, what about your livery customers, do you think any of them would be offended by it? We can soon set them straight if they ask for details I guess, we have nothing to hide now. At least I don't have to explain it to my boss!"

"Wow Carrie," said Dave, "I am amazed at your reaction, I thought you'd be really upset when Sally first showed it to me. You're becoming so strong, well done girl!"

Carrie smiled, "I am aren't I. It feels good. As for the article, it's something about nothing, I've faced worse. Caleb was a great diversion and has shown me I can appreciate a good man again but it's not real. My life is real and I am looking forward to it at last."

*   *   *   *   *

A few weeks later Sally came into the tack room with a magazine under her arm. "I thought you were giving those up," laughed Carrie.

"I'm trying, I've given up all the really trashy ones, this is a better quality one with proper interviews and things rather than sneaky photos and stuff. I thought, now you are moving on with life you might like to see an interview Caleb did about his future. It might help you find closure with your feelings for him."

Carrie thought for a second, "Yes I think I'd like that." Sally handed her the magazine.

The front cover had a beautiful image of Caleb, dressed in jeans and a hoodie looking out over some fields. Carrie had never seen him dressed in proper casual clothes and he did look good, even if he was a little too clean and well pressed to carry off the country look! The magazine was not one Carrie had seen before and Sally explained it was the celebrity equivalent of Vogue or similar. Carrie joked, "Is that why I haven't seen it in your collection before, not salacious enough?" Sally gave her a mock slap but she grinned.

"When I was in the shop, that front cover grabbed my attention so I splashed out, it was well over a fiver, you know. That's the main reason I never used to buy it, I like my salacious thrills cheap and dirty!"

After a good laugh, Carrie started reading the article she had found, with Sally looking over her shoulder.

Exclusive Interview - Caleb Kirkmichael explains "those" comments and the changes he is making in his lifestyle. With Angela Newburn

Angela: Good Morning Caleb and thank you for this interview. As I'm sure you know, since the Celebrity Awards last month, rumours have been rife about your future. I have heard you are marrying, you are dying, you are retiring, you are moving home. Of course, everyone wants to know who "Carrie" is and how she fits in with your new life. Can you tell our readers the full story?

Caleb: Hello Angela, thank you for offering to talk with me. I realised as soon as I had said those things at the ceremony that everyone would be twitching for news. To be honest I had a few drinks and I think my bravado got the better of me. I definitely regret mentioning Carrie – who is a special and private lady. We are friends and, although meeting her was a catalyst to the changes I am making, the changes themselves had been in my mind for about 5 years. So she is not to blame – she just gave me the courage to put things in motion. I'm so sorry Carrie if my actions have made your life uncomfortable in any way.

A: So you haven't spoken to her since?

C: Not properly Angela, that is why I am apologising to her here. I am not sure she wants me in her life right *now, I kind of dragged her into this crazy celebrity world without her permission and I should not have done that. Luckily no one but a close few really know who she is and it will remain that way, my lips are, belatedly, sealed, next question.*

At this point, Carrie didn't know whether to be mad or sad. Mad that what he said was true – although it had not occurred to her till then. But also sad that he may have been avoiding texting for fear of his reception. Never mind – it is all over so no harm done. She read on:

A: So the important bit for your fans – are you retiring from acting?

C: No – I love acting and it is in my soul – I will never voluntarily retire.

A: So what are the changes you are making in your life?

C: Well Angela. Since I was 19 I have lived the Hollywood lifestyle of hype and money. I realised about 5 years ago that it no longer made me happy. The ride has been an education and a blast, but it is time to get off the ride and find a place in the real world. If I still get offered roles in good films I will take them but I am disappearing from the social scene. I am moving out of America and generally giving up my 'playboy' lifestyle for something more fulfilling and meaningful. I am currently looking for a

property (I'm not saying where) and, as you know, my
Hollywood home is being sold. I am planning to spend
much of my time setting up a Sanctuary to help neglected
animals and much of my money supporting those animals.
This will be the last interview I do, unless the interview is
about helping my new cause, and I will no longer be
attending award ceremonies or publicity events to
promote my films. If this means the acting work dries up
then I will spend more time with my animals and be glad.
I hope that covers most of your questions as now I have
got that off my chest I feel the need to move on. All the
people who need to know my plans already know and now
your readers do too. Thank you for giving me the chance
to explain and for allowing me to do my last celebrity
interview. You have been most kind.

A: Wow thank you for that and one last question if I
may? ....Oh, he's gone! Caleb has left the room, he
obviously felt he had said all he needed to! Well, that may
be the last time we talk to Caleb Kirkmichael who is
obviously at a huge crossroads in his life. We wish him
well.

Carrie was smiling, with tears in her eyes and a
lump in her throat. Sally had put her arms around
her at some point although Carrie hadn't noticed.
Now she leant back in Sally's arms and cried and
cried. "I don't know why I'm crying," she sobbed.
"I'm so happy for him – what a brave move – no
going back now, he's told the world. He told me
some of his plans but I thought it would be ages

before he did anything. It must be a week for new beginnings, here's me feeling free from my grief at last and Caleb has kicked his career into touch to go find himself."

"You just cry Carrie, those tears are washing your slate clean! Soon life will offer you new opportunities to fill that slate right up again."

Carrie smiled at that thought. For the first time in years she felt truly free, life would be an adventure now, anything was possible – even love.

Text message from Carrie to Caleb:

Hi C. Great Interview last week. You nailed it – be happy. I have turned a corner too, feeling really positive about the future in both our lives. C. Xxx

Scary but good Matt!

Chapter 9

Laying out the chalk

Carrie was happy. Her life was getting back to normal now. And she was even happier that she had a proper 'normal' to get back to. Work was good, home was good and her stress levels and sadness levels were well under control. The upheaval of meeting Caleb had receded to being a happy memory over the weeks. She did not think of him much at all, just during every waking hour, and occasionally in her dreams! She believed that she had come to terms with him being her fantasy man rather than a real man. She congratulated herself on being able to separate fantasy from real life and just enjoyed the dreams. If she met someone new she was sure the fantasies would go.

Work had less routine through the summer and this week they were painting the stables ready for the horses to come into them for the winter. With rubbing down woodwork all morning and riding in the sun all afternoon Carrie was dusty and tired. She headed straight to her shower when she came in from work and put on her pyjamas ready for a quiet evening in. Once dinner was cooking (her turn to do the meal tonight) she sat down with a book. She finished work an hour or so before the lads, so she had half an hour's peace to enjoy.

As soon as she settled into her story her mobile began ringing from the kitchen. She swore under her breath then decided to leave it for voicemail, if it was important they would leave a message. She was just getting to a good part in her book when it rang again. Cursing, she went to fetch it.

The name on the screen was Caleb! She fumbled to answer, her heart racing.

"Hello."

"Hello Carrie, how are you?"

Her spine tingled and her hair seemed to stop fitting her head.

"Hi Caleb" (in a high pitched squeak – very cool!)

"Sorry to surprise you like this but I wanted to ask a favour."

"OK."

"Can I come round so we can discuss it?"

"You want to come here?"

"Well, yes, assuming you're at home?"

"But you don't know where I live."

"That's OK, give me directions from Sally's place, I promise no one is tailing me today! - or would you rather meet in a pub or somewhere?"

"No, no, here is fine. We're only about a minute from Sally's yard. Carry on down the main road through town. Take the second left and we are number 15 Church Road. When were you thinking of coming?"

"From what you just said, in about a minute. I am outside Sally's now. See you soon."

He hung up.

Shit, shit, shit, shit, pyjamas on, hair wet and messy, alone. OMG!!!

By the time Carrie finished her little meltdown, there was a knock on the door. She opened the door and hid behind it. Caleb bounded in looking amazing in jeans and a tight T-shirt. She slowly shut the door, feeling very self-conscious as she greeted him. His face lit up as he looked her up and down. "You look so sweet standing there all mussed, Oh – I didn't wake you up did I?"

She cringed as she shook her head – all ability to speak temporarily gone.

"Oh Carrie, I'm such an idiot, I was so looking forward to sharing my news with you that I didn't stop to think, I'm so sorry, shall I come back another time?"

"No, no, it's fine. If I'd had more warning I'd have put some proper clothes on and dried my hair but if you don't mind pyjamas then now is a good time," she smiled weakly.

"You look great, Pjs suit you," said Caleb.

"Shall we sit, would you like tea or coffee?" asked Carrie, hoping she could retreat to the kitchen to regroup.

Caleb sat on the sofa and declined a drink. Carrie sat on a chair opposite and tried to look relaxed.

"So, what's your news?"

"First tell me about your news," said Caleb, "your text sounded like you were feeling better about life?"

"Well, no huge changes but I am feeling better. I can remember Matt without getting sad all the time, and I'm getting my enthusiasm for life back."

"Oh Carrie, that's wonderful. I'm sure Matt would be proud of you."

"Do you know, I think he would. Now, tell me your news!"

Caleb leant forward, looking like an excited child. "I've decided where I want to settle and I have estate agents looking for suitable places for my Animal Sanctuary. I've contacted a few experts and got basic advice on what I need. I have three properties to go and view next week."

"Wow, that was quick work!" said Carrie. "Have you sold your Hollywood house yet?"

"Maybe, but that doesn't matter – I can buy somewhere without selling that."

"Oh to be so rich," joked Carrie.

Caleb looked a little abashed. "Sorry, I forget I'm lucky and not everyone can think like that. Anyway, these properties look hopeful and I'm so excited to go see them. They're in the south of England by the way, I want to settle here in the UK."

"I'm so glad things are moving ahead for you," said Carrie, totally shaken to hear Caleb would remain in England. "You mentioned you needed a favour? What can I possibly offer you?"

"Well," said Caleb, "I was hoping I could persuade you to come and see the properties with me. Firstly, I'd really value your opinion, especially about any horse accommodation. Secondly, I'd like to spend some time with you, and thirdly I really need to have someone with me who understands what I need. None of my other friends believe I'll actually do this and they'd only be interested in properties with swimming pools and posh entertaining rooms. I don't need any of those things any more. Will you come?"

Carrie sat and thought, her heart wanted to go, for at least two of the reasons Caleb had mentioned, she wasn't sure she knew enough to be much real help as a horse expert though. Was it a crazy idea? Would it just stir up her feelings and get her all confused again? Probably! Would she go? Probably!

"I'm sure you could find better advice than mine on horse accommodation, why don't you employ an expert?" she asked.

"I'll get expert advice on everything when I've chosen and bought a property, don't worry. However, I want it to be my home first and foremost so I need a friend to help me choose. I have the funds to make any property right, but I want the house, especially, to have the feel of a home as well as the room to build all the other things I'll need. This trip is about the heart of the place as much as its usefulness.

When we met it was like you 'got' me straight away, I hope you would 'get' the sort of place I need too."

Carrie didn't know what to say. "We've only really met a couple of times, how do you know I'll see what you need?"

"I don't, but I have a feeling in my gut that you will. Without wanting to sound desperate and sad, you are the best friend I have for the job! No one else I know will have the first idea what I want or need."

Carrie laughed. "So I'm the best of a bad lot am I?"

"That wasn't how it was meant to sound," he said, laughing with her. "When I tried to think who to ask, you were my first thought. Does that sound a bit better?"

"Much," she said. "How about a coffee while I think about it?"

As Carrie put the kettle on she heard the front door open and automatically prepared two more mugs of tea. She went back to the lounge and a weird sight met her eyes. Caleb stood with his hand out-stretched while Dave leant back on the door looking like he would swoon! Dave looked totally star struck and Caleb looked.....what? Confused? and a bit territorial? What was that about? She rushed out her introductions to ease the situation.

"Caleb, this is Dave, one of my housemates, Dave this is........OK, probably not needed."

Caleb had found his 'meet and greet' smile and looked more relaxed. Dave, if anything, looked even more like he would faint. They shook hands just as Carrie heard Gregg's car pulling up outside. Gregg came striding in and stopped dead when he saw Caleb, a similar, shocked look appeared on his face briefly, then he grinned and stuck out his hand.

"And this is Gregg, my other housemate," said Carrie.

Gregg and Dave gave each other a hug and kiss and Gregg winked at Carrie.

"Tea's brewing," she said – as if that made everything normal.

As she went to fetch the drinks she heard Caleb saying. "So you both live here with Carrie? She told me she had housemates but I'd just assumed they were girls. To clarify, you two are a couple and Carrie is single, right? I don't want to misunderstand anything!"

Dave, who was still brain dead with shock, nodded in agreement. Gregg hugged Dave and said,

86

"Yes that's right, we needed somewhere to live about 2 years ago, saw Carrie's advert in the local shop, and here we are, it works well."

"It started just as a means of paying my bills," said Carrie, coming out of the kitchen, "but we've become such good friends, it's like I went from being an only child to having two brothers, I love it - and them," she said smiling at the lads.

"So I hope your intentions are honourable with our little sister," Gregg laughed. "Or else...."

Carrie groaned at that comment and Caleb laughed, "Duly noted," he said, "it's good to know Carrie has back-up, although she seems very good at looking after herself."

They all sat chatting and laughing for a while. Caleb told the lads of his new plans and they discussed films a little. Carrie realised she needed to give Caleb an answer to his request for her help. Somehow having Caleb here, chatting with them all, made the whole idea a lot less scary, it was only a short trip away after all.

"Lads, I need your opinion on something, Caleb has asked me to go down south to look at properties for his new home and animal sanctuary. If I can get time off work should I go with him?"

Both lads said, "YES!" in unison.

Caleb looked surprised but smiled. "I'll take good care of your little sister and bring her back safe and sound. My intentions are honourable I promise."

Carrie added, "Whatever his intentions, we will be going as friends and nothing more, if that's OK then I would love to go with you Caleb – as my brothers approve!" She winked at the lads.

Caleb looked so pleased, she felt guilty for delaying her decision till now.

"What day are we going?" she asked him.

"I hope to find more properties while we're there so I think we should stay down there from Tuesday to Friday," Caleb replied. "I didn't mention this bit before, because I wanted the decision to be yours, but I dropped in on Sally earlier and she'll happily give you the time off. I told her I was coming here to ask you. She said to tell you you should go! She also said she expects photos."

"I feel deeply hurt that you did that," Carrie said, although she was grinning broadly, "but as long as I get my own hotel room and don't have to pay for it I'll be there."

"That goes without saying, of course I'm paying

for everything, you're doing me a huge favour, just bring yourself and your advice, and those Pjs which are really growing on me!"

Carrie blushed a little and asked, "Will you pick me up or shall I get the London train and meet you there somewhere?"

"It will be door to door service madam, I'll pick you up here at 8am Tuesday morning. Travel light, bring what you wear for work so we can get grubby poking around farms and something cleaner for evenings but please don't worry about what to wear, everything will be casual, that is my new rule in life. No more penguin suits for me."

After a few more minutes chatting Caleb said, "I have a night of filming ahead so I'd better get going, it's been great meeting you Dave and Gregg."

Carrie saw him to the door and stepped outside with him for a minute. "Thank you for inviting me," she said, "It'll be fun. A chance to help spend that much money isn't likely to come my way again!"

Caleb smiled. "Thank you for agreeing to come, it means a lot to me."

He kissed her lightly on the cheek and said, "See you Tuesday, and I promise to behave, think of me like another brother." With that, he jogged to his car and waved as he drove away.

She smiled to herself and thought - *Another brother, yeah right, that will work!!*

Is this OK Matt?

Chapter 10

Up in the Air

As she re-entered the house Carrie realised she was shaking and grinning. The lads were talking nineteen to the dozen but went silent when she appeared. "What?" she asked, as if she didn't know. Both lads jumped up off the sofa and surrounded her in a big cuddle.

"He is totally into you," said Dave dreamily.

"No he's not, he's just glad to find someone who understands his love of animals. All his showbiz friends think he's making a big mistake, this isn't about me at all."

"Honey I love you," said Gregg, "but sometimes you are totally thick when it comes to romance!"

"Bloody cheek, brother dear," she replied.

Dave added, "He is a gentleman and a patient man, but he is soooo into you – and I do mean in 'that' way before you say he is just a friend."

"Well I'm not interested in 'that' way so we can just be friends, can't we?"

They both fell about laughing at her comment. "You **are** so interested in 'that' way," said Gregg. "You can fool yourself but you can't fool us!"

"But I am not ready for 'that' yet," she cried.

"Oh, I think he's shown he will wait," said Gregg.

Carrie went up to her room to think. Should she be going if the lads were right? Would it all end up in more heartache? No, they can't be right, they are just looking for a fairytale where there isn't one. I can control this and enjoy it without any strings, I think?

* * * * *

Tuesday came round so fast.

She had spent far more than she could afford on some new jeans and a top for the trip. She would take her least scruffy work clothes too but she needed the confidence boost of something new for evening wear. She bought new underwear too, practical stuff, not sexy stuff, as no one would see them, but still, they gave her confidence. Sally had been so excited for her and they had spent the week discussing property pros and cons like they were buying it for themselves. Sally had advanced her a bit of pay and gone shopping with her for the clothes. They both felt like giddy teenagers by the end of work on Monday night.

The lads were equally giddy and teenager-like, with advice on romance in general and hooking Caleb in particular. It didn't matter how many times she told them to stop they couldn't help imagining she would be the new Mrs Kirkmichael by Friday.

At 8am precisely there was a knock at the door. Dave was nearest and answered it with Carrie seconds behind. Caleb stood there in tight jeans and a hoodie looking very hot. Both Carrie and Dave's hearts fluttered a little.

Dave greeted Caleb and invited him in. "Hi Dave, good to see you but I won't come in. If you are ready Carrie we should get straight off – our transport is parked in a 'no waiting' zone."

This confused Carrie. "There aren't any 'no waiting' zones in Elver," she said.

"I know," said Caleb, "but I promised I wouldn't leave the chopper sitting on the rugby ground for more than half an hour, it tends to dent the ground a bit and the groundsman was getting twitchy."

"Oh my goodness, a helicopter," squeaked Carrie.

"Yes and a cab is waiting to get us there so shall we go?" He took her holdall and headed out the door, smiling to himself at Carrie's reaction.

"I play at that rugby club – I hope he hasn't pissed them off," said Gregg, coming out the door to say goodbye.

"Don't worry, I had permission to land, I was just asked not to stay too long. I've promised them a donation and some signed stuff for their next fund-raiser, it's only the groundsman who was worried. I'll send him something nice too."

As Caleb got into the cab a man Carrie didn't recognise walked past. He glanced at Caleb then looked again, pointed, realised what he was doing was a bit rude and hurried on. She heard Caleb say "Good Morning" to him as he scurried away.

Carrie hugged the lads and joined Caleb in the cab. "Did you know that bloke?" she asked.

Caleb laughed. "No, but I get used to people thinking they know me, occupational hazard I'm afraid."

"That must be weird," she said

"It's OK in the UK, most people are a bit more reserved about it, but in the US it is a nightmare, everyone wants a piece of you," he answered.

"Happy house hunting guys," Dave called as they pulled away.

They reached the rugby club and found a few people had gathered, intrigued by the big chopper. The cabbie was able to drive them right to the doors of the helicopter but Caleb turned and waved at the small crowd and shouted, "Thank you for letting me land." Once they were inside and strapped in, the pilot started the engines and the big rotors slowly picked up speed. Carrie had never been in a helicopter before, she was nervous and fascinated in equal measure. The pilot had given them headphone things to wear and she found she could hear both him and Caleb talking through them. They discussed the weather conditions and flight time. Caleb turned to Carrie and asked if she was comfortable, she nodded. "You can talk too, we'll both hear you at present but the pilot will isolate himself once we take off so we can chat privately. I hoped we could study the property details while we fly?"

"OK," she said, her voice echoing in her head and sounding strange.

"In the US I have a pilots licence and my own chopper but I am not licenced to fly here so I hired us a chauffeur. I'd love one of these twin-engine machines, more speed and a bigger range. We're about ready to take off, do you need to hold my hand, you look freaked out?"

"I'm OK," said Carrie, "but a hand would be nice." Caleb shuffled as near as he could get to her and took her hand to his lap.

"If you watch we're going to fly out over Sally's yard. We'll be high enough not to upset the horses and she said she'd look out for us going over." Carrie felt a little lurch as they left the ground and then Elver started to spread out below them. She could see the people on the Rugby field getting smaller as they rose almost straight up. Then they turned and headed out towards Sally's. She looked down and could see the horses in the far fields. They seemed unworried by the chopper, thank goodness. As she watched they headed over the house and yard. She could see some movement and hoped it was Sally waving at them. After a while she stopped recognising the landscape and turned to Caleb. "Wow that was sooo exciting!" she grinned.

He squeezed her hand and reached into his bag for some paperwork. The estate agents details were in the usual format with a photo and some info on the front and more photos and in-depth details inside. "How shall we start this?" he asked. " I've read all of these so often I could probably perform them like a script! I guess it would be better for you to read them and give me your opinion after?" Carrie agreed and settled back to look at each one. She tried to see beyond the words, everyone knows estate agents only tell you the good bits.

Two of the houses were fairly grand, all had age to them, and one really just looked like a home for a farmer with no frills. They all had in excess of 100 acres of land, some arable, some grazing land and some landscaped as garden. One had a small wood, two had big ponds or lakes and all had ranges of farm type buildings. The one that looked like a farmer's home had a courtyard with stables and old cart sheds around the back door. One of the others had a lovely range of older, stone built buildings as well as some new portal barns. They all looked to have the potential he needed, if money was no object. They were all 'Price on Application' which she knew meant if you have to ask you probably can't afford it!

"Caleb they all look exciting but I need to know what animals you're planning to keep? Some of the natural features, like a pond or lake, would be good for a swan sanctuary but could be a waste of land and possibly a danger if you're keeping herds of horses. Can you tell me more about your plans?"

They spent the rest of the journey discussing what Caleb's dreams were. It seemed he wanted horses to be the main animals, with dogs and other pets catered for as the sanctuary took shape. Although he didn't want to specialise in farm animals, he knew if a sad case came to light, he would take them too. He hadn't thought about waterfowl but as he said, if the pond is there, they can come.

"I plan to have a resident Vet on site eventually and people experienced with rehabilitating animals so some can go on to have new homes and good lives. I do not want to be a sanctuary that just hoards animals, I want the expertise around me to get the animals healthy and happy then find them loving homes. All I can bring to the sanctuary is money but that money can enable good people to do good work. I want to learn and be hands on as well. I've never allowed myself to have pets as my life has involved travelling so much. Now I want to immerse myself in animals 24/7."

"So are we looking for a place with extra houses on site to house staff? It might be easier than getting planning permission, rural councils have a reputation for blocking what they might consider a housing estate going up. Have you had any advice on what areas are likely to be supportive to your plans?"

"I hadn't really thought that through, planning in the US is different to here. I'll get my lawyers onto it if we find a potential site. See, you are already more on the ball than me and we haven't reached the first property yet. And you thought you wouldn't be a help. We should be to the first property soon, I'm really excited," said Caleb.

"Which one is first?" asked Carrie.

"One of the ones you described as 'grand' so maybe we won't like it." Moments later the pilot patched into their headphones and announced that they would be landing within 10 minutes.

"I got the estate agent to arrange a landing site on each property and have it made visible from the air, I don't want us to worry any livestock, or squash any crops." Within a short time, they were descending towards an empty field near a big house. The gardens looked huge and immaculate, and Carrie spotted lots of outbuildings dotted around behind the house.

Carrie was glad to get out of the helicopter and stretch a bit. As she looked around a suited gentleman appeared from the house smiling and waving at them. Caleb stood beside her and watched him approach. "This should be the agent – Andrew, let's see if he really understood the type of property I want, as you said, this doesn't look like a working property, it's a bit neat and tidy."

"Welcome Mr Kirkmichael, madam, please let me show you around." The agent took them straight to the house, a small, Georgian Mansion with eight bedrooms. The inside was very spacious and extremely well presented but, as far as Carrie was concerned, it had had the soul totally ripped out of it. She said this to Caleb quietly and he agreed. Very quickly Caleb asked to move outside and look at the outbuildings. Whilst the two big barns were in good condition they did nothing to inspire Carrie. They were fitted out almost as an extension of the house with tile floors and painted internal walls. One barn housed a small collection of classic cars and the other housed a light aircraft.

The smaller stone outbuildings nearby were fairly untouched and full of cobwebs and junk. These were the best bits of the property by far for Carrie but they needed waterproofing in a few places. Caleb sensed her excitement for the old rundown stone buildings and whispered, "These are cute but they don't make up for that house!" She had to agree. "Can we speak to the owners?" asked Caleb after a while, "I'd like to know more about the type of land they have."

They headed back to the house and found a couple in their forties waiting to greet them. Caleb introduced himself and Carrie, he asked what they did with the 120 acres that came with the property. "Oh we don't do anything with it personally, we rent it out to two local farms and they grow crops on it or something. They want to buy it all but we were advised to keep it with the house until we see if buyers want it. I understand you do want land?" Caleb looked a bit disappointed. "We do want land but I'm afraid the house is not what we were looking for at all, thank you for allowing us to see it though, and good luck with the sale!"

The three of them headed outside and Andrew followed them to the helicopter. "Come aboard," said Caleb, "so we can chat." It was cosy in the chopper with three in the back and their bags, Carrie found herself struggling to concentrate with Caleb so close beside her. "So this obviously wasn't the house for you," stated Andrew. "What did I get wrong, do you want a grander house? I thought I had understood that you wanted modest accommodation but I can find grander for you."

Caleb and Carrie looked at each other and laughed. "Quite the opposite Andrew, I want less house and more outside stuff. I really wanted to see working farms, as I told you. I could change this property to suit me but I want to find one that grabs me from the start, one with a heart. Try to forget what you know about film stars and find me some practical places if you can?"

"OK, I think I understand. The second property I had planned to visit today has a very similar feel to this one. How about you forget that one and see the third one this afternoon, if I can arrange it. Meanwhile I'll look around for more suitable properties. The third one was booked in for viewing last, on Thursday, because I thought it might be too 'agricultural' for you but it seems I was off the mark! Give me half an hour and I'll rearrange the viewing for later today."

"Sounds good," said Caleb. "We'll find a pub and have lunch, probably a daft question but is there anywhere near a pub we can leave the chopper while we eat?"

Andrew laughed. "Not a question I get asked a lot, to be fair, but if you hold on I'll ring my father, he has a paddock you could land in and there is a good village pub nearby. The ground is so dry at present it should be perfect." Andrew made the call and soon they were ready to take off. Andrew showed the pilot where the paddock was on a map and then headed there in his bright red car so the pilot had a visual clue where to land. Once the pilot had cleared the short flight with local Air Traffic Control and done his checks they were off.

In a few moments they were hovering over Andrew's suggested field. He was there waving them down. The pilot had a good look all round for obstructions as they flew by, then hovered low and checked the ground. He was obviously happy as he gently set the big beast down. Andrew and his father approached as the rotors stilled. There were introductions all round and much handshaking. Caleb thanked Andrew's father for his hospitality and asked both if they would join them for a meal.

He also asked the pilot, but he had sandwiches and fancied a snooze in the sun. They left him happily leaning on the undercarriage and enjoying the fresh country air.

The pub was a lovely old building with rendered uneven walls and Carrie just knew it would have beams inside. She even forgave Caleb when he said it was 'Quaint'. They ordered from the menu behind the bar and found a big table by a window to sit at. While they waited for the food, Andrew rang his office to get his colleagues searching for suitable properties. Meanwhile, he checked other local Estate agents for their listings as well, he knew he could negotiate with them on commission if one of their properties fitted the bill. He had already arranged their afternoon viewing for 3pm so they had a few hours to relax and enjoy the surroundings.

Their meals arrived, the waitress spending far too long leaning over Caleb as she delivered his plate. "Good old fashioned pub grub," Andrew's father said, tucking in. Caleb was a little subdued so Carrie quietly asked if he was OK. He smiled. "Yes, just a little disappointed that the first one was an anti-climax."

"Let's look at the listing for the next one and remind ourselves what it has," suggested Carrie. "I think it was my favourite when I read the details before, it had a lovely old courtyard at the back that was so pretty. And the house was right in the middle of the land which makes it feel like the heart of the place I think." They asked Andrew to pull the details up on his laptop so they could look at the photos again while they ate. The house was not big and it seemed much more lived in than the last house but Carrie loved the feel of it. The field that had been photographed to illustrate the land looked like it had been grazing land forever. It was surrounded by mature hedgerows and had a pony grazing in the shot. "This one does look more like the rural idyll I have in my head," laughed Caleb. "Let's hope it lives up to the photos."

They rejoined the conversation of Andrew and his Father, which was on properties that might be for sale in the area. "How close are we to the next property?" asked Caleb. "Could this be my local?"

"Not really," said Andrew, "it's in Santon, about 25 miles away, but there's a pub near it and a village shop. If you look at the map it is right on the coast, some of the furthest fields are on the cliffs. It's actually a very popular part of the area but still very rural."

Andrew's Father piped up, "We had a house in Santon when we were first married and loved the place with young children, it hasn't changed much, they haven't let the developers ruin its charm like some places. It has a great little shop for essentials and a very pretty church. The farm you are looking at is about a mile or so out of the village, very rural indeed." They finished eating and sat for a while chatting. Andrew had to return to the office so he took his father home, saying, "See you later". Carrie and Caleb sat in the pub garden and talked about life. "What made you choose this area?" Carrie asked. "I assume you could have settled anywhere?"

"Strangely, I was born near here, hence my mostly English accent. We didn't move to the US until I was 14, so I have fond memories of this area. I first revisited, as an adult, about ten years ago and kind of fell in love with it again. There is still so much open space and greenness. I love the local building stone and the way the old buildings seem to blend with the countryside. I also wanted to be near the sea, so this next property definitely ticks that box. I like London for easy travelling but the pace of life seems more natural here. I'm so done with the frantic pace of life in the US – or at least in the bits I know. My parents still love it there but I'm happy to return to my roots."

Carrie smiled, she liked his answers, they said a lot about the new man he wanted to be. "So, you're English by birth, that's a surprise, despite your accent, I thought that was an actor thing and you chose the accent that fitted your company. I like English Caleb by the way, you sound very smooth and debonair."

"Thank you, I think! I love the variations in accent here but my natural English is a bit public school as I was a boarder until I was 14. Believe me, life in the US was a huge culture shock after a boarding school in rural England." They chatted on for an hour before it was time to head back to the helicopter and visit the next property.

Still with me Matt?

Chapter 11

Finding "The One"

As they landed in a cute little paddock Carrie looked around at the property. It was obviously a working farm, there were old rusty farm implements buried in the hedgerows and fields of grazing cows in the distance. There were two big portal barns nearest to them, nearly hiding the house, with its selection of old stone buildings, that they had spotted as they flew in. Even with just a view of steel barns the place felt good. There was a long drive leading from the road through the fields to the house and Carrie could see tractors and newer implements sitting in the nearest barn. She could hear and smell animals. This property had a heart. Caleb was looking around and smiling too. Maybe she did know what he needed?

Andrew appeared from near the barns and came over to them. He immediately started to apologise for the mess, saying he had asked the owners to tidy up this area for their arrival. "But they weren't expecting us here for another two days," said Carrie. "Anyway, I think this is normal for a working farm, don't you Caleb?"

"It looks fine to me, I can see past the odd bit of scrap metal," said Caleb happily. They made their way towards the house, sneaking a look at the barns as they passed. The second barn was fitted with animal pens, empty in summer, but ready for the cows in winter, Carrie guessed.

When they came round the end of the barn they got their first look at the house. It was lovely. The courtyard that they had seen in the listing was bigger than expected but gave a wonderful cosiness to the house nestling along one side. The outbuildings making up the other two sides of the courtyard were long and low and matched the stone of the house. There were stables and other pens, an open-fronted cart shed and opposite the back porch of the house was a two-storey building that could have been a small mill maybe or a hay store. As they entered the back porch of the house Carrie noticed a line of wellington boots against the wall, she knew, seeing the boots of all things, that if she was choosing, this would be her home. They went through the back door straight into a lovely farmhouse kitchen. The cabinets were fairly modern but they had an aged feel that fitted perfectly with the Aga that stood in an old hearth. Caleb took a deep breath and visibly relaxed. They wandered around the rest of the house and were not disappointed. It was all a little worn and lived in but it was a home. Caleb was inspecting all the nooks and crannies and beaming to himself. Andrew just stood in the lounge and watched, surprised and delighted that Caleb was smiling.

"I'm going out to the outbuildings," Caleb suddenly shouted from the kitchen. Carrie rushed out to join him. They poked around every pen and stable with growing excitement. "What are you thinking?" asked Caleb suddenly.

"It is amazing, if I could buy it I would," laughed Carrie.

"There is a lot of work to do out here but these buildings are wonderful. Do you think I could make the two-storey bit into accommodation for staff? It's locked so I can't get in to see.

"It would probably be perfect if the planners approve, but there is plenty of room around the big barns for expansion if you wanted to keep this part private – it's quite close to the house."

Caleb grinned, "So not only do you 'get' me totally, but you're still giving me ideas that I would never have thought of, I think you've earned you bed and board and it's only the first day!"

"Glad to be of service, boss," she replied, winking.

"To be honest, if the land looks good, I think we may have found 'the one' already, but I guess we should see what Andrew comes up with next?"

"That would be the grown-up thing to do," said Carrie.

"Being grown-up is overrated but I'll try it," said Caleb happily.

Andrew appeared out of the house with a man they hadn't seen before. "This is Mr Bernard, the owner of this property, Mr Bernard meet Mr Kirk-michael and his friend Carrie."

Handshakes were shared and Caleb said, "Do you have time to drive us around the land Mr Bernard? We're keen to see it all and I'm guessing Andrew's sports car will not survive an off-road excursion."

"I'll get the Land Rover out and I can take you round," said the farmer. With Caleb in the front and Carrie and Andrew in the back of the scruffy old Discovery, they headed off away from the yard.

Each field they passed seemed well fenced and some had cattle in. A few fields were obviously being left to grow for hay or silage and one or two looked to have already been cut. "Is there water piped all around the farm?" asked Carrie. "I can see troughs in most fields."

"Yes, we have water even in the far fields, as we graze them all at times."

"Does being so close to the sea cause any problems for livestock?"

"The furthest fields are right on the cliffs but we don't suffer from coastal erosion here as the stone is very hard and dense. Further up the coast where the stone is softer, you can wake up after a storm having lost half your field into the sea! It can get mighty rough and cold on the cliffs in winter though, so we usually bring the stock nearer the house, easier to keep an eye on them too. They graze those cliff fields all summer and Autumn with no problem."

"Do you have sycamores on the farm?"

"Only one or two down along the road boundary I think, why?" asked Mr Bernard.

Carrie replied, "All parts of the tree can be toxic to horses and the seeds spread so far that they can be present in grazing acres away. Knowing there are not hundreds of those trees here is a big bonus. Do you control things like ragwort and hogweed?"

"Yep, we spray when necessary, docks tend to spread well here so they get sprayed off too so they don't take hold."

"Thanks - I must say your grazing looks good and clean."

Caleb had been listening and learning as Carrie asked questions. "Mr Bernard, are you including any of your machinery in the sale?" asked Caleb.

"I'm open to negotiation – I am retiring so I won't need any of it, but I'm not about to give it away!"

"What about the scrap implements – are you going to remove those?" asked Andrew pointedly.

"I was planning to take them to the scrappy before you got here, then you arrived early."

As they finished talking they drove through a gateway and up towards the front of the house. Having only seen it from the back they were impressed by how pretty the front of the property was. A huge pond dominated one side of the front drive, with ducks bobbing about on it. The other side was mostly fenced as a paddock but the area right near the house was hedged off as a sweet little cottage garden with such beautiful flowers and shrubs.

As soon as they returned to the courtyard Caleb said, "Thanks for the tour Mr Bernard. We will go and discuss what we have seen. We have other properties to see tomorrow so hopefully we will let you know either way by this time on Thursday. Andrew will contact you if we have any other questions. Goodbye for now, and thanks again."

With that, Caleb got out of the car and walked off towards the helicopter. Carrie and Andrew followed. Caleb didn't speak again till they were in the chopper.

"Phew, sorry about the quick exit, if I'd stayed any longer I would've made him an offer here and now. It's so like the place I had in my imagination, it hurts to walk away."

Carrie was grinning from ear to ear. "I'm so glad you felt that strongly. It's the most wonderful place. Can I come and work for you?" she giggled.

Andrew was looking at them both with a confused but happy expression. "This job always surprises me, I think I can judge what people will like, then every now and then someone totally throws me. I had expected you to hate this one, expected you to like the first house. Maybe I need a new career!"

Caleb laughed. "No, you've found my dream home in only two tries, don't quit now, you're good! Did you find any others for us to see? I feel the need to be rational and thorough, even though I know I will end up buying this one."

"We searched the whole area and the only other farm of this type we found is under offer already, we could view it but it may not be available, unless you made them an offer they couldn't refuse?"

Carrie said, "Of course that's Caleb's decision but if I was the one who made the first offer then some-one else gazumped me I'd be heartbroken, it's a horrible practice."

Caleb put his arm around her and squeezed her to him. "I'm so glad you said that, and I agree, I won't do that to someone. I'll go with my heart and buy this one. I need to talk to my lawyer and my accountant and check a few details but I'll ring you tomorrow Andrew, probably with a firm offer for Mr Bernard. Please don't tell him yet, just in case there is a problem."

Andrew nodded, said his goodbyes and walked back to his car via the house.

Caleb asked the pilot to take them to their hotel in the nearby town, apparently the hotel had it's own helipad, amongst other luxuries. As they both sat back and strapped in Carrie felt a twinge of sadness, she might never get to see this special place again. She looked out the window, memorising the sights and the feelings, just in case. Caleb was talking to the pilot through the headset but she wanted a minute to think so she didn't put hers on. Soon they were flying over fields and roads towards the town and the hotel. Caleb patted her leg and motioned for her to put her headset on. When she did he asked, "Are you

OK? You're very quiet."

She smiled. "Yes I'm fine, and happy that your dream is taking shape for you. What a roller coaster ride today has been!"

"We can rest for a while at the hotel then we can eat and talk about our little farm. I was right about your empathy, you and I were definitely on the same page today. It was a wonderful experience, thank you for coming." Caleb leaned over and kissed her lightly on the forehead. Before she realised what she was doing she leant sideways and rested her head on his shoulder. He didn't move away so she relaxed and breathed in his musky smell as she closed her eyes for a second. "Our little farm, our little farm......" Carrie drifted off into a nice little fantasy world. When she opened her eyes again they had landed, "Hello sleepy one, do you feel better for the nap?" Caleb's soft voice bought her fully awake.

"I'm so sorry, I must have been more tired than I thought. And yes I do feel better, thanks."

"Right, let's get ourselves settled in our rooms then later we'll chat, I'm bursting with excitement and I need to go back over what we saw. I need you to explain all those questions you asked Mr Bernard and I want your ideas for what to do to the farm without spoiling its charm. Is that all OK? Do you need to sleep more first?"

"And breathe," she suggested. "Let's get settled then we can chat. I don't need to sleep but I do need a cup of tea!"

Caleb had a quick chat with the pilot and then they made their way into the hotel. They registered and Caleb asked for someone to fetch their bags from the helicopter, he also ordered tea for two in their rooms. True to his word Caleb had booked them separate en-suite rooms, but they formed part of a big suite so they also had a shared sitting area between the rooms as well as a big balcony over-looking the golf course.

Carrie sat in her own room and thought about their day. Was it really only 10 hours since she left Elver? It had been one hell of a ride! Caleb was in his room showering so she decided to do the same, whilst trying not to think about him naked and just the other side of the suite. All sorts of emotions had been awakened today – raw and real emotions – not just her little fantasies that she had been dismissing for months. Strangely she felt a sense of calm. She was still not ready to act on them, even if Caleb was interested in that way, but she accepted they were there and wasn't so worried by them. She was sure Caleb liked her as a friend and that would have to be enough. Hell, it was amazing, he had seen the world and had people throwing themselves at him for years but he chose to spend these 4 days with her. What a confidence boost from a man so out of her league that they should never have even met! She knew her life was back on track emotionally after the years of grief and she would find a new partner one day. It didn't feel like betraying Matt any more, she knew he would want her to be happy. If she never saw Caleb again after this week she would forever love him for showing her that.

Still Love you Matt, I am going forwards again.

Chapter 12

Onward and Upward

Carrie came out of her room 20 minutes later, clean and in her new jeans and a pretty purple top. Caleb was just pouring the tea. He smiled and handed her a cup. "Hi, you look refreshed and lovely," he said sweetly.

"Thanks. They have amazing showers, I'm used to a half-hearted trickle of water at home but I feel pressure washed after that."

Caleb smiled. "Can we talk through the day now, I'm bursting to brainstorm so I can justify buying the place!"

"Ugh, I hate that word," she laughed, "can we just have a civilised chat over a cup of tea?"

"Which bit did you like best?" smiled Caleb. "Which bit gave you the first 'feels' for the place?"

"That's easy, I loved the rusty implements and the cows grazing," she laughed, "but those bits aren't staying so that's not much help."

"It helps a lot, it was the first impression when we arrived and that's important. We both seemed to take a breath and relax when we saw the fields we landed in. We couldn't even see the house from there but we both reacted positively to the view. I could see my sanctuary there in my mind."

"That's true," said Carrie, "and nothing we saw after really changed that feeling for me. I would love to live in a place like that. The house kind of hugged you as you walked in and the old outbuildings were perfect for poorly animals needing watching through the night, or for your own animals if you have any. With the kind of funds you say you have, to nurture the old buildings and put up new ones, I can't see a downside really. Not many people could afford to renovate all that but it sounds like you can? Don't overdo it though, the 'feels' need to be protected, if you see what I mean?"

"I do see, once again you prove what a good team we make,I've been planning sympathetic renovations in my head since we left. It's definitely going to be my home, I **am** putting in an offer in the morning."

"You sound so sure, it must be the right place, I'm so pleased for you."

"I am sure," he said, "I've been paid obscene amounts for my work for 20 years. With investments and good advice, I have more than I can possibly spend before I die! I even recently tried supporting a couple of struggling small film companies by bank-rolling their films and acting for just a stake in the profits. I thought there would be no profit, and blow me if both films didn't break box office records and net me more than my usual fee! It's time to make all that money work for me and my animals now, instead of just being frittered away on a fake life.

Going back to the farm, I think I'll work with what's there first and build more as I learn what I need. I could probably have twenty horses there tomorrow, with the barns and the courtyard for the winter stabling. The rest can grow organically as we find out what animals need our help. I'd like a few home comforts in the house before I move in, I've been spoilt over the years! Could I cope with twenty horses if I had, say, one clued-up staff member to help do you think? I don't want to rush into getting staff but I do want to start taking in animals as soon as I can."

"Yes, no problem, Sally and I cope with twenty-three between us at present and you are not likely to need to exercise many of the rescued horses, which is a big chunk of our workload. How will you find the right person to help?"

"Well.....I was wondering if you might consider taking on the job? It will probably be at least four months before I can move here as I have one more short film commitment after the one we are finishing now. I don't plan on having any animals here till I can be here full time and there will still be work to do. So there is no hurry to decide, you probably have nearly six months to think about it, but I know we could work together after today, and your experience would be invaluable to me. Please think about it? Don't make a snap decision though, I can wait."

"Wow, what a great offer, of course I'll think about it, I'm no expert but I know when to call one in!" Yet again Carrie's thoughts were thrown into turmoil. They chatted on for hours about the farm and Caleb's plans. Somewhere in the middle they ordered room service and ate. Finally, around 1am, they said their goodnights and went to their rooms.

The next morning Caleb was up and making phone calls long before Carrie surfaced. At around 10am she woke to a gentle knock on her door. "Carrie, there is a pot of tea out here, shall I pour you a cup?"

"Yes please," she called as she threw on her new clothes and went to wash her face. When she emerged from her room Caleb was on the phone talking to someone about the farm.

"That was my English lawyer," he said, "who's starting the conveyancing today. I have spoken with someone from another animal sanctuary, I met them

121

years ago, she is going to come and look at the farm, once it's mine, and advise me on getting started. I have phoned Andrew with a good offer for Mr Bernard and my accountant is working out which of my investments to take the money from. And all before you lifted your pretty little head, how's that for a mornings work?"

"Scary to be honest, but wonderful," she smiled. "When will you hear back from Andrew?"

"Any time now, with luck. Andrew was heading out to the farm as he knows Mr Bernard doesn't carry a phone with him when he's working. I asked for a price for all his machinery too, I'll find someone to look it over for me when he gives me a price."

"So we can just sit here and wait for the call that will change your future forever, that will be so relaxing," she laughed.

"I know, I don't think I even want breakfast until it's settled. I'm too nervous."

Within 10 minutes the call came through. Mr Bernard had accepted Caleb's offer and would work out a price for the machinery. He was keen to have three months to sell his cattle and move out so hoped Caleb could complete in September. Caleb asked to be allowed access to the farm to get builders quotes and take measurements over the next few months and thanked Andrew for all his help. As he ended the call Caleb danced around the room with glee, he grabbed Carrie and they danced together like crazy people. Eventually, they slowed and Caleb took Carrie's chin in his hand and kissed her lips. She responded to his kiss just a little before pulling away and looking down. "Thank you so much for sharing this with me, Carrie, I hope we get to share again soon." His soft voice made her wonder if he meant the kiss, but she was sure he meant the farm, he was just in high spirits.

Carrie searched for something to say to break the moment. "What will we do now, we can't view more properties and you seem to have covered all the 'making it happen' stuff. Are we going to head back to Elver today?"

"Do you want to go home?" he asked quietly.

"No, I'm having too much fun," she grinned, "but the chopper and the hotel must be costing a packet and we've already achieved what you wanted to do, going home would be the grown-up thing to do."

"Well, we stay then, I love it when you're less grown-up, you look so carefree. I forgot to say, I sent the chopper home last night as we had finished house hunting, he'll come back for us on Friday if we want him to. We can hire a car or just explore the town on foot. Whatever you like, now I know this is going to be our local area I am happy to learn all about it."

"Ooh shops, sorry that sounds very girlie, and I have no money anyway, can I change it to, Ooh sightseeing?"

"We can do shops and sightseeing," he said, laughing, "we have three days to explore, and I'm partial to a little girlie shopping myself, but don't tell anyone!" They ordered breakfast and got ready to hit the town.

Matt, are you still with me?

Chapter 13

Learning

Walking towards the town centre Carrie and Caleb were still chatting about the farm. "Did we find out what the farm is called," asked Carrie, "I must have missed it on the estate agents details."

"Its name is Cliff-top Farm," said Caleb, "I'm happy to keep the name or change it, what do you think?"

"I'm not sure, it's not a bad name but maybe you should think of something more memorable for the sanctuary. We could look on the land registry website and find out if it has always had that name, if it's historical you might want to keep it, but if it has already been changed then it wouldn't seem bad to change it again."

"Clever and pretty, just how I like them," quipped Caleb, as he dodged a friendly slap!

They reached the town centre and happily browsed along the shopping street. "Oh my goodness," Carrie suddenly stopped, "we didn't take a single photo of the farm, Sally will kill us."

Caleb grinned, "I've been racking my brains to think of a reason to go back there before we leave and now we have one! I will phone Andrew now and ask him to arrange it for tomorrow. We can spend a few hours looking around and planning if Mr Bernard doesn't mind. Great thinking Carrie."

"Can we take some video too – will my phone do that? I'd love to keep it as a memento."

"Great idea, and yes your phone can do that." Caleb phoned Andrew and asked him to arrange the visit as they stood there in the street.

They carried on walking, stopping to window shop here and there. Carrie didn't want to go into the shops as she really had no money and didn't want to be tempted. Caleb found a country clothing and saddlery shop and decided he needed some new boots as he was going to be a farm owner. They looked at all the wellies and yard boots and he chose a very expensive pair of brown Nu-buck long boots that were very 'Country Life' looking, a far cry from the battered old pair Carrie wore to work in. "You won't want to get them dirty," laughed Carrie.

"Can I buy you a pair too?" Caleb asked.

"No, I'm happy in my comfy old boots, they still

have plenty of life in them, thanks though."

They passed from the shoe department into the saddlery and browsed for a while. "You will need some of this stuff, in time. So it's good to see there is a shop nearby," said Carrie.

"I'll need help when the time comes, it's all a bit confusing to someone who rides on film sets and to relax but has never owned a horse." They paid for his boots, arranged for them to be delivered to the hotel and carried on down the street.

Carrie stopped to read the small ads in the saddlery window. Caleb carried on but stopped a couple of shops along and looked in the window. By the time Carrie caught up he was moving on again with more purpose. "Shall we find a quiet coffee shop he asked?" Carrie nodded and they took a side street that led down to the beach. Along the front, there were a few coffee shops to choose from and most looked busy. "How about we get take out and sit on the beach? It'll be easier to talk than in a noisy cafe." Carrie agreed, they bought coffees and headed onto the sand. It wasn't really warm yet so there were not many people on the beach. They sat on a little ridge of sand and watched the waves while they drank.

After a few moments, Caleb looked at Carrie and said, "We need to talk." He looked very serious.

"Have I done something wrong?" asked Carrie, worried.

"Oh Carrie," he smiled, "what I want to talk about is us, me and you, what the future holds for us. Oh sod it, I'm just going to say it - I have tried to hide it but I am totally and utterly in love with you. I tried to hold it inside, doubted myself and my motives, tried to be patient and let you find me, tried to think of you as just a friend but I can't. I know I should give you more time, and I would wait forever to let you heal enough to love me back. I thought I could get my life sorted while you healed and then ask you to be with me but I can't bear the thought of missing my opportunity – of losing you. Yesterday made all my feelings sort themselves into place. I love you."

Carrie stared out to sea with tears in her eyes.

"See, I knew it was too soon for me to tell you, I should've kept quiet, waited, but I can't be here all the time, I have to go back to the States in a few weeks. I didn't want to come back in a couple of months and find you had moved on without me, found a new partner. Please Carrie, I want us to share our futures, do you think you might love me one day? I can wait, we don't have to rush anything. I have wanted to love you since that first night, but I told myself I was not worthy of loving anyone then, told myself you were not someone I should be with until we were both ready for forever. I'm ready for

forever with you Carrie.............Please say
something!........................."

"I'm ready," she whispered.

"You're what?"

"I'm ready to look forward to forever with you, if
you will have me. I'm not ready to do much more
than look forward yet, but I know that will come. If
you can be patient with me and we can make
changes slowly then I'm ready for forever with you."

Caleb was quiet and Carrie was afraid to look at
him. Slowly and tenderly he lifted her chin to look
into her eyes. She was crying silently. He closed the
space between them and kissed her lips so gently it
hurt. She kissed him back and they were still, eyes
closed, their foreheads touching and their breath
mingling, as the waves broke and the gulls cried.
"I'm so in love with you Carrie," he whispered.

She opened her eyes and looked into his. "I've
been denying it to myself for weeks but, I love you
too Caleb."

His eyes filled with tears and she gently kissed
them away.

They held each other in a long and gentle
embrace, listening to the gulls and each other's

hearts. Caleb finally broke the silence hugging her tighter and turning to look across the waves.

"We have so many things to learn about each other, I need to tell you about my past and the things I've done that embarrass me now. I don't want you to hear the truth, or the lies, from anyone else. I hope there is nothing that would make you change your mind about me. I want you to know that I'm no longer that person and going forward I will do nothing that could hurt or embarrass you. I have never felt like this with any other woman. I have had many relationships, and many liaisons that don't even deserve that title, but I have never met anyone until now who shared my soul. I wish I could erase my past when I am with you. No one else has ever made me feel I want to be a better person, just for them."

"Oh Caleb, I will never judge you on your past. Who can truly say they would have acted differently, given the same circumstances? I love who you are now, and your past taught you to be that person, so don't regret it for anyone. I don't think I have any secrets to tell you, but I may need to talk about Matt as I carry on healing and I know that might be hard for you."

"Matt helped form the woman I fell in love with, I have no jealousy towards him, just gratitude."

"I might cry again now," she smiled weakly.

"Maybe we should both thank him for bringing us here?" said Caleb. "Let's do it loud and proud."

"THANKS MATT," they both shouted.

The last ghost of a doubt in Carrie's mind smiled and moved on.

THANKS MATT!

Chapter 14

Refilling the slate

As they finally stood up off the sand and walked towards the road Caleb said, "I have a shop I want to go back to before we do anything else, if that's OK with you?"

"Fine with me, do they sell chocolate – I think I need some!"

"No, but we can do that after." They strolled back to the shops and wandered along hand in hand. Caleb stopped outside an expensive looking jewellers. Carrie stepped away looking worried, "I thought we were going slowly."

"Carrie I want the world to know you are mine, I want us to have rings as a symbol that we are together forever. We can call it an engagement or anything you like. It can last for years before we go any further, but when I'm away I want us both to have a symbol of how we feel for each other. If that is too much then I understand but please, if you can, let us do this?"

"OK."

"Just OK?"

"Now I understand why you want to do it, it's OK. I like it. Here's the truth that might put you off me though. There is no way I can afford to buy you a ring, I wish I could but unless we can win a plastic one in the amusement arcades across the road I just don't have the money – I had to borrow the money for the clothes I'm wearing!"

"Oh Carrie, I am so insensitive, forgive me. I can't believe you had to borrow money for new clothes to come away with me, it wasn't supposed to cost you anything, but I didn't think it through. Of course, you wanted something nice to come away in. I didn't expect you to buy me a ring either, I wanted to buy us both rings, that match, so we belong. I didn't think about you wanting to buy mine, and I am sorry if I was an idiot. Will you let me do this?"

Carrie suddenly giggled, "Was that our first row? If so, bring it on, it means we are a couple now! Let's get in there and buy us some rings."

Caleb breathed a sigh of relief and grinned as he followed her into the shop.

Carrie smiled at the assistant and asked, "Can we see some matching 'his and hers' rings please, I think we might be getting engaged." Caleb hugged her from behind and kissed her neck, "That sounds sooo good."

The assistant smiled at her, looked up at Caleb and went pale. "I'll....... get the manager." He scuttled off like he had seen a ghost. "Do you ever get used to that?" she asked Caleb.

"I hate that people feel uncomfortable around me just because they have seen me at the cinema. I hope he comes back so I can make him feel at ease."

The assistant did come back, with the manager. "How may I help you sir?" asked the manager.

"Well firstly my fiancée was the customer, but we would like to see some 'his and hers' ring sets please."

"Of course Madam, Sir. My assistant will bring us the selection, umm....do we have a price range?"

Caleb nonchalantly replied, "Not really."

Carrie turned a giggle into a cough and put her hand to her mouth. Under her breath she said, "smooth, playboy." Before they had recovered their composure the assistant returned with a tray of very expensive looking diamonds. Carrie looked at the rings with concern. "Don't forget I spend most days mucking out stables. I want a ring I can wear all the time but I don't want to be worrying about it all day. Can we look at cheaper ones?"

Caleb's hand reached out to the rings and picked a pair before she had a chance to look at them. He asked for her hand and tried it on her finger without showing her the ring. It felt like it fitted perfectly, he removed it gently and hid it in his hand. He then tried the men's ring on himself, still hiding it from Carrie. His ring was a little tight but he got it on judging by the look on his face.

He turned to the manager and asked, "Platinum?" The manager nodded.

He turned to Carrie and asked, "Do you trust me to pick a ring you want to wear forever?"

Carrie nodded eagerly, intrigued by his speed of choice and slightly turned on by his becoming so masterful!

"If mine turns out to be too tight can you size it up for me?" A nod from the manager.

"Can you engrave them inside this afternoon?"

"My engraver will be here in the morning, I can have them done by lunch tomorrow."

"OK, we'll take them, but I want to have them tonight and bring them back in the morning for engraving."

"That's fine sir, I'll box them for you."

"Thank you, my card." Caleb handed his credit card to the manager. While the payment went through Caleb turned to the young assistant and grinned. "Thanks mate, write down your address and I'll send you some signed merch from our new film. If you and your boss want to take a photo for the shop wall you are welcome, just don't tell people what we bought if that's OK, I don't want Carrie hassled by the press."

Caleb posed with both men for a few photos in the shop and then he picked up the bag with the rings in and took Carrie's hand. "Shall we go sweetie?" Outside Carrie reached up and kissed him, "That was some performance, you should consider acting as a career." Caleb laughed and put his arm around her as they walked.

"I saw the rings when we first walked down the street and dared to hope I could buy them for us. They just looked so right sitting there in the window, beautiful but practical. Platinum is harder than gold so they should survive a farming life!"

"When do we get to wear them? I can't wait."

"We are going to find a car to hire then we are paying a little visit to our farm. We won't be expected so we may have to make do with sneaking in for a few minutes to exchange rings but I'm sure we can think of an excuse if we get caught!"

"Perfect, our farm. Do you know, when we left there yesterday I said goodbye to the farm in my head, in case I never saw it again. I was so sad. Now I can be happy to say hello again."

"I love you Carrie, even if you talk to farms in your head!" Within half an hour they had returned to the hotel, arranged a hire car and were driving towards the farm. Caleb had hired a shiny new Range Rover so they could drive around the farm easily on their authorised visit the next day.

As they approached the farm they decided to follow the road that the farm was on and see where it went. The road seemed to follow the line of the farm frontage for a few hundred yards then veered away along the coast. As the road turned away from the farm boundary Caleb noticed a track on the left that continued following the fence line of the farm. They turned down the track and followed it for a while. They came to an open gateway that Carrie remembered from yesterday's drive around. They were now on the land they were buying. They carried on for a few yards and suddenly came out onto the top of the cliffs, the sea lapping gently below them and the sun shining above. "This is a good place I think," said Caleb, stopping the car.

They jumped out and walked a few feet from the car. Caleb turned to Carrie and went down on one knee. "Carrie will you make me the happiest I have ever been by agreeing to marry me – when you feel ready of course – no pressure."

"I will my love, I will." He smiled and slid her ring onto her finger.

She finally got a proper look at it. "Oh Caleb, it's lovely. I knew I would like it but you really chose well." The ring was a thick band of platinum which bulged organically at the front to surround the large diamond. There were no claws on the setting and the stone was held by the platinum all around its circumference. The appearance was a cross between a very modern setting and a medieval design and was very simple but beautiful. "Can I put mine on too?" he asked.

"Give it to me please," she said, getting down on one knee too. He laughed and passed her his ring. "Caleb, will you spend the rest of your life with me in your heart?"

"I will, of course, you beautiful, crazy woman." She slid his ring on, with difficulty, they stood and she lifted her face to kiss him.

The kiss started gently, slowly becoming more passionate as they held each other. Eventually, Caleb broke away hesitantly. "We need to stop now if we are keeping things innocent my lovely. Parts of me haven't got the memo about going slow!"

Carrie smiled and backed off a little. "Thank you for loving me Caleb."

They sat on the grass, at the cliff edge, barely touching, but totally together. "This place is magical," sighed Carrie. The sun was going down and the sea was tinged with orange. "Life here with you will be magical too."

Caleb sighed, "I feel like my life is starting again, in the right place and with the person I was meant to be with. Are you sure you are going to be OK living here, so far from your friends and your old life?"

"I have never been more sure of anything, and they will visit – who could resist afternoon tea with the one and only Caleb Kirkmichael?"

As they headed back to the car they decided that eating a late lunch would be a safe and chaste occupation. After a classy meal of fish and chips, which Caleb didn't think he had tried since he was 14, eaten while sat on a bench on the prom, they returned to the hotel for a restful evening. Caleb raided the minibar for the chocolate they forgot to buy earlier and they chatted about the farm.

Carrie was worried that Caleb might want to do more than chat after such a monumental day but she knew she needed time to adjust. To her frustration, she found he was almost too respectful of her wishes and they even sat on separate chairs all evening! They didn't kiss again until they went to their own rooms to sleep. "Night Caleb," she whispered hugging him close.

"Night my sweet, sleep well." They kissed deeply and Caleb pulled away first.

"I am going to have a shower, a very, very cold shower! Sweet dreams Carrie." he winked and shut his door behind him.

Matt?

Chapter 15

Back to reality

Thursday evening found them in the helicopter flying back to Elver. They had a wonderful day on their new farm, photographing every feature and videoing a drive around the land. They had dropped their rings into the jewellers to be engraved and, true to his word, the manager rang them before lunchtime to say they were ready. Annoyingly, Caleb would not tell Carrie what was engraved within and had packed the rings away, saying, with a grin, that he should ask for her 'Brother's' approval before they wore them again.

They decided Wednesday evening that they would head back Thursday after their farm visit. It would be too frustrating being so near the farm for another day and not being able to visit. Caleb rang the helicopter company before Carrie realised what he was doing. When she said he was extravagant he laughed. "Things will change soon but for now let me treat us – I loved watching your face every time we took off."

Caleb had been on the phone a lot Wednesday

evening. He disappeared into his room for some of the calls, saying he had work stuff to discuss. She even missed his presence when he was right next door, how would she cope when he returned to the US? He had suggested she go with him, but she knew she couldn't let Sally down by asking for so long off work.

The two of them now sat leaning against one another just enjoying the closeness and the view as they flew up the country. Carrie was wondering how much she would see of Caleb now they were heading back to reality. She knew he still had a bit of work to do on the English film and he said he would be going back to the US in a few weeks. She suddenly felt sad, "How long have I got you for before you go away?" she asked quietly.

He hugged her tight, "We shouldn't worry about that today, and I have no work till after the weekend so let's not think about it yet."

"I wish we had stayed in the hotel for another night, I didn't think about not seeing you all the time till now."

"I can be all yours in Elver just the same," he said.

"That's good, but I love having you all to myself, my silly brothers will be around now!" pouted Carrie. He laughed.

Very soon they were circling Elver and preparing to land at the Rugby club. At least this stop would please the groundsman – the chopper only touched down for long enough for them to disembark, luggage in their hands. They waved as the pilot took off again and walked to the road. "No cab this time," rued Carrie. As she spoke a familiar jeep appeared at the roadside and Sally jumped out waving madly. Carrie rushed to her friend and hugged her tight. "I've missed you Sally, have you come to pick us up, did you see the chopper coming over or were you just passing?"

"I had a heads up that you might appear this evening," she said grinning at Caleb, who tried to look innocent.

"How are the horses?" asked Carrie. "I have missed them all, even crabby Peggy. Oh and Terry too of course."

"They're all fine, nothing exciting has happened, all is well."

They threw the bags in the boot and Sally drove them to Carrie's house. "We have great pictures of the farm Caleb bought," Carrie said, "can you come in and look?"

"I wouldn't miss it for the world, Terry's at home so he can keep an eye on the yard."

As they approached the front door it was opened by Gregg. "Oh – did you have a heads up too?" asked Carrie.

"When we knew you were going away we took a couple of days off – to enjoy ourselves without our little sister around. Typical of you to come back early and shatter our peace," Gregg laughed, hugging her. Dave appeared behind Gregg and said, "Welcome home Carrie, kettle's on, who wants what?" They filed into the house and settled to chat. Caleb sat beside Carrie and discreetly put his hand on her back as she chatted with Sally and Gregg and caught up on their news.

"How was the trip? Did you find a property?" asked Dave, carrying a tray of drinks out of the kitchen.

"I did," said Caleb, "and we have pictures to prove it, can we connect my phone to the TV and show you?" Dave reached for the phone to look then opened a drawer under the TV and found the right cable. He soon had the first photo on the big screen. "There are some videos on Carrie's phone, can we see those too?" asked Caleb.

"Sure can – phone, Carrie?" She passed it across.

First, they looked at the photos. Sally was really interested in the barns and the courtyard and asked lots of questions. The lads were more interested in the house and came up with loads of interior design ideas. Everyone agreed that the place had a lovely homely feeling. They watched the videos of the trip around the land, admiring the sea views and the layout of the fields. When everything had been viewed Caleb said. "We both fell in love with the place within two minutes of getting out of the chopper. It was just right. The estate agent was very confused, he thought I would want a posh mansion, not a scruffy farm! I put in an offer the next morning and it was accepted, the place should be ours by September."

"The farm looks lovely but I'm sure you have some other news, I could hear it in your voice Caleb, when you rang to see if we would be here tonight. Come on, spill – what's with the 'we' and 'ours'?" Gregg was looking between Carrie and Caleb smiling.

"Yeah, Caleb asked me to bring a big bottle of champagne," said Sally. "I hoped it was about more than the farm."

They all looked at Carrie for confirmation. She grinned sheepishly and said, "Well.... we might have accidentally got a little bit engaged while we were under the influence of that gorgeous farm!!"

Squeals of delight filled the room as Sally and the

lads jumped up to hug them. "I knew it, didn't I tell you before you went that this would happen?" squeaked Dave, jumping for joy. Gregg and Sally just smiled and hugged till Carrie and Caleb felt like their ribs would break.

"Does this mean I have permission to marry your little sister chaps?" Caleb laughed. "We don't want to do anything in a hurry but it **will** happen, when Carrie feels ready."

"Permission soooo granted," said Gregg, "as long as we are invited – Dave is still looking for an excuse to buy his new dress!" Dave pretended to look offended, but couldn't keep a straight face.

"Can we get a glass of the champagne that Sally mentioned?" asked Carrie. "I feel the need."

Sally dashed out to her car and came back with a cold box, inside were two bottles and loads of ice. "I couldn't find a big bottle, there's not much choice in Elver Co-op, so we have two normal bottles." Dave had rushed to the kitchen to get glasses. As Caleb opened the first bottle and poured, Sally asked, "Do you have a ring yet Carrie?"

Carrie turned to Caleb, who smiled, "We had our private moment to get engaged on the cliffs of the farm but I thought we might do a replay for our friends." He pulled a box out of his pocket and got down on one knee in front of Carrie.

"Carrie, will you make me happier than I have ever been by agreeing to become my wife?"

"I will my lovely."

Cheers from the audience

Carrie asked him for his ring and got on her knee again.

"Caleb will you keep me in your heart forever."

"I will my love."

More cheers

They both turned and bowed to the audience.

"It went something like that, and then we kissed," she said, reaching for Caleb and looking up invitingly. He held her tight they kissed deeply.

"Awww so cute," said Dave, hugging and kissing Gregg.

"Enough you guys," laughed Sally, "I'm feeling like a spare part here." They all grabbed a glass of champagne and sat.

Gregg raised his glass and said, "To Carrie and Caleb." The others joined the toast.

Suddenly Carrie squeaked, "The inscriptions, I nearly forgot – can I look Caleb? Oh, I don't want to take it off now." Caleb took her hand again and gently removed her ring. He held it out so she could read what was engraved inside.

It just said 'Our Cliff-Top' and had the date that they got engaged, the same date that the offer on the farm was accepted. Carrie smiled and said, "It's perfect, I guess you decided not to change the name then?"

"I felt that whole day was 'our cliff-top', emotionally and literally, we could finally see our future spread out before us. So yes, the name stays."

"I love you Caleb." She snuggled into him as he replaced the ring on her finger. They forgot they were in company for a moment until Gregg said, "Ahem - More champagne anyone?"

Much later Carrie and Caleb were nestling on a tiny sofa in her little private lounge upstairs. They had been quiet for a while when Caleb said, "Carrie, can we talk about money?"

"What do you mean, my lovely?"

"I can't bear to think of you struggling along with next to nothing when I have so much. I know how independent you are and I'm proud of you for that, but can I help you now that we are together?"

"I don't know."

"Can we think of a way to make it right for both of us? So I can relax knowing you aren't struggling and you can accept the help without feeling guilty about it."

"Do you worry about me financially then?"

"So much, right from the first time we met, it seemed so unfair that I had more than I need and you had to struggle to live. I didn't know how to help then, without seeming brash or insulting. Now I know all my money will be yours to share when we marry, so why can't we share it straight away?"

"A marriage doesn't always mean shared wealth though, I was going to suggest a prenup so you knew I wasn't a money grabber."

"There is no way in this world I would agree to that – we are going to be equal in all we have. I don't want a business deal, I want a lover, a wife." With that Caleb kissed her soundly as if to seal the deal.

She thought about it all for a while and then said,

"I want to carry on working with Sally until we can go to the farm. If I'm leaving her, she needs to get someone trained up to replace me. If you could pay me a wage, maybe for helping arrange the farm renovations in my spare time, she wouldn't have to pay me. Then she could afford to pay a new person straight away and she can get them trained before I leave. I don't need much."

"I'm not paying you a wage to be my fiancée," he laughed, "but I can put enough money in your account so you can afford work for free, if that's what you'd like to do?"

"It sounds like a plan. I'll try not to spend any more than I need to."

"Please Carrie – spend loads, buy new clothes, buy yourself a car, a horse, anything. I want you to feel what it's like to be free from money worries. If I told you how much there is in my accounts you would not be feeling guilty about the little bit you could spend."

Be happy for me Matt.

Chapter 16

Towards the Cliff-Top

It was a few days since they returned from their trip. Caleb had stayed at a hotel in Elver until Monday morning, visiting with Carrie during the day and going back to the hotel late at night. If the lads were surprised by that arrangement they kept quiet. She had offered Caleb the sofa bed in her little lounge but he said he needed to be away from temptation at night. She felt guilty as she knew she was nearly ready to take the next step, just not quite.

Carrie felt they had really got to know each other over these days and she felt secure and blissfully happy having Caleb in her home all day. She was worried that he would be bored but he seemed to absorb the peace of simple home living as if it were all new to him, and it probably was. She looked forward to a time when they could share their farm home, they could make it a haven from the stresses of the world outside.

Caleb returned to his film work on Monday morning, promising he would drive out to see her any night they got finished early enough. He was getting a train to London at 8.30am so they had said their goodbyes Sunday night. Carrie was glad she was returning to work, she needed to keep busy. Sally was waiting for her with a mug of tea and a hug when she went in at 8am. They sat in the sun in the stable yard and caught up on recent news. Caleb was transferring some money into her account that morning so she paid Sally back the money she had borrowed for clothes, she felt better for doing that. Sally took the money and said, "So, when are you leaving me then?" trying not to look sad.

"I have a plan," said Carrie, "but I'm not leaving for a few months anyway, unless you want to get rid of me?"

Sally looked relieved. "I will miss you when you do go, but I'm so happy for you both, you deserve this."

"Sally, how would you feel if there was a way you could train up a new assistant while I was still here to help out?"

"That is just not possible Carrie, I can't afford two wages."

"I know, but there is a way you wouldn't have to, can I run it by you and see what you think?"

"OK, I'm all ears!"

"Caleb is determined to give me some money so that I'm not struggling any more. We talked about it for ages, as I wasn't sure I wanted it at first. Anyway, as I can't live at the farm, for a few months at least, I want to stay here and still work with you. I love it here and I will miss it so much when I leave. I know you'll need a new assistant when I go so I thought I could work for free. I'm to be a kept woman, and you could use my wage to get someone else started. We could train them in your strange ways together! Will you let me do this for you as a thank you for taking a chance on me when I was so low?"

"Oh my, Carrie, I don't know, I need to think about that. It doesn't seem right somehow. But it is very tempting, just to keep you here a bit longer! Oh and talking of losing friends, I had some sad news last night. Bilbo is going up for sale and is likely to leave the yard. Not only are his owner's good payers but I am very fond of Bilbo, he's my favourite to ride, as you know. I hate to think of him being sold to someone who doesn't take good care of him. I don't usually get this attached but there is something special about that gelding."

"Oh Sally, I know you love him, I can see it when you ride him - and you give him extra treats when you think I'm not looking! I'm so sorry, I will miss him too."

"If he were mine I could choose who to sell him to

so I knew he was OK, it sucks not being able to see where he goes. Mind you, if he was mine I wouldn't part with him anyway!"

"Can't you buy him Sally?"

"Terry said I could, but I need to be a business-woman about this, I don't need him for the business, in fact, I do need his space here to earn me money. I don't have enough stables or grazing to keep horses here that don't pay the bills. Sadie is my only exception as she is too old to sell and I love her to bits."

"You are right of course, but what a horrible position to be in, let's hope he goes to a good home, I'm sure he will."

By now they were getting ready to start painting stables, as they talked. Sally took another look at Carrie's new engagement ring before she covered it in a glove. "It's so lovely," she said, "simple but elegant, did you see the price tag?"

"Sally, I'm shocked," said Carrie laughing. "Sadly no – but I'm sure neither ring was cheap, I could see pound signs in the jeweller's eyes as he saw which ones Caleb chose!"

"Whilst I'm shocking you, can I ask how much of a kept woman you are going to be?" Sally grinned deviously.

"Oh Sally, really!" Carrie said, in her best shocked voice. "If I'm honest, I don't know. I gave him my account details and he said he would transfer some first thing this morning. When I said I would try not to spend too much he got all domineering and said I must spend it, suggested I buy new clothes and stuff!"

"Do you have internet banking on your phone? Can you look now?" Sally asked.

"Yes I do and no I can't!" Carrie laughed.

"Oooh the suspense is killing me – please look – pretty please?" Just as Carrie decided maybe she should look, her phone pinged with a message. It was from Caleb.

Hi beautiful, I miss you. I have transferred some money and set up a monthly payment so you have the same amount every month. If you need or want more, just let me know. Please buy yourself something wonderful, it will make me happy. I'll ring you later when I know if I can get back tonight. Love you. C xxxxxx

When she had read it twice she sent a quick reply.

Hi C, missing you too. Thanks so much, I will check it arrived safely. All my love. C xxxxxx

Turning to Sally she said, "It's your lucky day, I need to check the money arrived in my account, I might show you if you are good." Carrie found her banking app and went through the login process. When she reached her current account she gasped. Caleb had sent her twenty thousand pounds. OMG, it must be a mistake, surely. She texted him straight away.

Hi C. You have sent me £20k did you add too many zeros? £2k a month would have been plenty. Shall I send it back? Love you. C xxxxxx

Sally was wriggling with curiosity beside her but she needed to get this sorted before she showed anyone. His reply arrived.

Hi Carrie. Yes it is £20k, no mistakes and the correct number of zeros. DON'T YOU DARE send it back, I know people who couldn't make that last a week never mind a month. Spend the damn stuff, enjoy it, KEEP IT!!! p.s. I am laughing so much I just fell off my chair.
Love you sweetie. C xxxxx

Carrie turned to Sally and showed her the text. "I think he's a keeper!" was all Sally could say, having read it. The women just looked at each other in shock for a few moments.

Suddenly Carrie shouted, "BILBO," at the top of her voice. Sally nearly hit the ceiling, she was so startled.

"What, where?" Sally looked around, assuming the horse was charging towards them.

Carrie giggled and said, "I have missed having my own horse, I am now stupidly well off and I love Bilbo, why don't I buy him?"

"Oh my goodness, would you? Can you? Is he what you want?" asked Sally.

"How much are they asking for him?" asked Carrie.

"Around four thousand I think, with all his tack and rugs."

"Is he worth it," asked Carrie, "or should I offer less? It's years since I bought a horse."

"Well, he's a good little jumper but too small for big competitions. He schools well enough but isn't really a dressage prospect. He is a good hack or hunter really. I think you should offer £3500. Or do you want something you can seriously compete on? He would be great for local shows, but he won't take you to Olympia or Badminton."

"I want a hack really, I have no wish to compete or hunt."

"Then he would be perfect. Let's get him saddled up and you can take him out for a try. I'll come out on one of the others that need exercising." They abandoned their painting and were soon tacked up and heading out across the fields.

"Can we head up the hill and round the road so I can see how he behaves?" asked Carrie. Sally agreed and headed that way.

"This is the ride we followed on your interview, if I remember correctly," said Sally.

"Yep. It seems so long ago. I will miss riding with you Sally."

Sally smiled sadly and hastily said, "If I remember rightly I was on Bilbo that day and he wasn't very confident when a lorry came past. You'll be glad to hear he is much calmer in traffic now, he was only 6 years old then and not very experienced. He must be nearly 9 now. The girl who owns him has taken him to riding club rallies and local shows and he behaves well."

"Why is she selling him?"

"I think she's lost interest a bit, she is 17 and has a boyfriend. She doesn't come and ride him that often now."

"Should I get a vet to look at him before I decide?" Carrie asked.

"Normally I would say yes, but he's been here three years, if there was anything wrong with him I would know by now, so it seems pointless really."

They reached the hill and Carrie set off at a fast canter to the top. Bilbo was lovely to ride and very keen to go. She could see why Sally liked him. After the hill, they headed back around the road through the town. Plenty of big vehicles passed them and Bilbo remained calm and sensible. When they returned to the yard Carrie rode into the arena to see how Bilbo was in there. He was willing and worked well for her. "How come you have never asked me to ride him before? He's amazing," said Carrie.

Sally looked a bit embarrassed. "I kept him for myself, I love riding him."

Once they had turned the horses back into the field Sally asked, "Well, do you like him? I would be so happy to know he was with you."

"He's absolutely lovely, for the first time in my life I'm going to be impulsive and make them an offer. I know I can afford to keep him here till the farm is ready, so he doesn't have to cope with two moves either."

Sally was suddenly crying and Carrie hugged her. "I'm sorry, I am so relieved, I have put so much work into that little horse because I liked him so much. I think he will be your horse of a lifetime – he is special Carrie. Thank you."

"Let's get on the phone to his owners and make them an offer they can't refuse," said Carrie.

Sally went inside to make the call, Carrie was too nervous to listen. Within 10 minutes Carrie was the owner of a horse. "They accepted £3500 when I told them it was you buying him, they were happy he could stay here and they know you are experienced and kind. They will be up at 6 tonight to collect the money and bring you a receipt and his passport. All his tack and things are here already so you can look them over. He has good quality stuff, they have plenty of money."

"I think I need another cup of tea," said Carrie, "I'm not used to being so impulsive."

While they had a brew Carrie asked Sally if she had thought about letting her work for nothing. "I phoned Terry and asked his opinion while I was in the house. He said it was up to me but just to check the insurance as you are not really an employee if I don't pay you."

"I would really like to do this if we can. If it suits

you I could have the freedom to have some days off, if there are things to arrange for the farm, so it would give me the freedom to help Caleb too."

"OK, if we can do it, we will, and you can have as many days off as you need, of course. Could you check the horses in the far field while I go and phone the insurance company to see where we stand? I will start advertising for a new yard assistant as soon as I can."

"Yep and I'll text Caleb, tell him all the news, and ask him for a raise, I am getting good at spending his money!!"

Hi C my love. You'll be proud to hear that your money had hardly hit my account before I spent 3.5k of it on something I really didn't need, but love! Sally will love you forever too, because he is her favourite livery horse and she was dreading him being sold to someone who wouldn't look after him properly. He is called Bilbo and he is a lovely 9 year old cob, well built and with a great character. I hope you can forgive my impulsiveness but Sally was crying thinking of him going, and now he can stay till we go to Cliff-Top. She is over the moon and I am too. Thank you. Cxxxxxx

P.S If you come back tonight you can meet my second new man this week!

Caleb replied.

Hello sweetie, I'm amazed and delighted, I'll be home by 5.30. It might be the last time I get back to you this week so I'll be there come hell or high water. This new man had better watch his step, I don't do threesomes!! We have our first animal for Cliff Top! It will feel even more like a home now. Looking forward to meeting Bilbo. Is he big enough for me to ride too? C xxxxxxxxx

Hi again. Bilbo would carry you easily but your legs might look a bit long on him. He's not very tall – a bit like me! C xxxxxxxx P.S. Don't worry I won't be sharing you with anyone!!

Caleb's final text was just a line of laughing emoji.

Nearly healed Matt.

Chapter 17

Ready in 'that' way

As Carrie expected, Caleb fell in love with Bilbo as soon as he saw him. "He is a short chunky boy, I feel less jealous now. If he had been tall and lean I would have thought you were trying to replace me," Caleb laughed.

"He's not that short, he's 15 hands according to Sally." Carrie was already defending her new man.

"However tall he is, he is very cute," Caleb said to make up for his joking.

At 6pm the owners arrived, hugged Bilbo good-bye and exchanged a receipt and his passport for a cheque from Carrie. Now Bilbo was properly hers. Sally and Caleb stayed in the tack room out of sight but ready to congratulate her when the old owners had gone.

As Caleb and Carrie headed home Caleb said, "My timetable for the new film is changing and I have to go away sooner than expected. We will wrap up here by Thursday if we work all hours and nothing goes wrong. I have to fly to the US on Friday morning. You know you are welcome to come with me, don't you? I do understand that you don't want to let Sally down though."

Carrie tried to look calm, but she must have failed.

"Aww, I'm so sorry sweetie," said Caleb, "I don't want to go but I can't let people down either. I have decided after this next gig I'm not taking on any new film stuff for a year, even if it's offered. I want time with you. We need time to get our farm up and running too."

"That sound's good, and I do understand about not letting people down, will I see you again before you go?"

"I was wondering if you would come down and stay with me Thursday night, and see me off on Friday? I will send my driver to pick you up and he can make sure you get home safely on Friday too. I can get you your own room so no pressure or anything."

Carrie smiled and looked coy, "Ummm, about that. If you are going away for sooooo long maybe I would like to...... ummm....... 'share your room' before you go? I feel ready, I think, as long as we......."

Caleb stopped walking and took her in his arms,

she could feel the tension in him. He whispered in her ear, "Carrie you are amazing, I will be so careful with you. I will make you feel so loved. We can part knowing you are truly and completely mine and I am truly yours." He let her go and said, "Now we need to walk further apart or I might make you 'truly mine' right here on the high street!"

They returned to Carrie's house laughing.

*   *   *   *   *

Later, before Caleb returned to London for the night, they sat chatting in the big lounge. The lads had gone to the pub. "Carrie I hope you don't mind but I have given Dave some money to buy you a laptop for your room. He is going to set it all up with Skype and a camera so we can see each other when we talk while I'm away. I know it will feel like such a long time and I need to see your smile every day."

"Wow, thank you, that will make things so much better. I did wonder if I could come over there for a few days once Sally's new assistant is settled in?"

"Great minds think alike, I was going to suggest that too, will you be OK travelling alone?"

"As long as you can meet me at the airport I'd be fine."

"Wonderful, we can look forward to that. Hey, I can take you to meet my parents. I haven't said much to them yet, I was waiting until I saw them so they understand you are for keeps, not another in a long line! I told them about looking for a farm and they thought it was just a phase I was going through! They laughed!" Caleb looked like a hurt child for a second, then recovered and smiled ruefully.

"Caleb, thank you so much for giving me time before we got too intimate, I know it has been frustrating for you."

"Carrie, I would wait forever if it was necessary, I have never felt like this before but I want everything we do together to feel perfect and natural. I have always thought sex was the reward in a relationship, but with you, the reward is our happiness. If I knew we could never make love I would still be here. My physical attraction to you is very strong but my emotional attraction is what makes me see our future. Please don't feel pressured to do anything till it is right for you. The cold showers are working, mostly!"

"I love you Caleb, you say the best things, let's make Thursday night something special to remember when we are apart. Just to put your mind at ease, I am totally physically attracted to you too, and also feeling frustrated, but the grief and pain I have felt has made me scared to take risks. I trust you and I trust myself to be yours completely, but I am still scared."

"I understand, and I will take so much care of you." He reached for her with so much love in his eyes. They came together, his left hand behind her head holding her as his tongue gently explored her lips. She opened her mouth to him and returned his heat with her own exploration. Caleb's mouth moved down her face and onto her neck, placing soft kissed down her throat and onto her collar bone. She moaned softly, kissing the top of his head as her hands held him tight. His hands travelled down her back, stroking and caressing every inch. He moved his mouth back to her lips then gently pushed his tongue deeper into her mouth. She stroked his tongue with her own causing him to groan from deep in his chest. His hand reached her curves at the base of her spine and he gently tucked his hand into the waistband of her pants, cupping her bum and causing a deeply satisfying feeling as he pushed her hips close to his. She breathed in his musky smell as his passion increased, losing herself in the heat it created in her mind. She could feel just how aroused he was and could feel herself losing control. This felt so right......

With a groan and a sudden backward movement, Caleb pulled away and stood up. He sat himself at the other end of the sofa and regained his composure. Carrie sat where he left her, panting slightly and feeling frustrated.

"Sorry Carrie, I nearly lost the plot there. That was amazing."

"We can carry on if you like," she said, but despite her arousal, she was suddenly also fearful.

"We are waiting for Thursday, I'm not giving in to my urges now after being good for months. And anyway, by then, we will both be so frustrated that nothing will stop us," he grinned.

"I'm not sure how I can work tomorrow," grinned Carrie, "I'll be thinking of your lips and hips all day. I might have to kiss my other new man instead!"

Caleb grimaced. "And now I'm jealous of a bloody horse!"

"I need to go my lovely," he added, "we have to work like crazy to get this film finished before I go to the US and I need my sleep – after another freezing cold shower of course."

"I'll see you Thursday then, what time will your driver get here?"

"I will tell him 6pm, that way you will have time to relax after work. If we are working late he will bring you to the studio and I can show you around.

If we've finished by then he will bring you to my hotel. I will make time for us whatever happens, I love you Carrie."

"I love you too Caleb. I'll text you tomorrow."

They said goodbye at the door with a rather chaste kiss and Caleb drove himself away.

*   *   *   *   *

The next two days were torture for Carrie. She alternated between feeling sexual frustration, total abject fear and deep love. The whole switchback of emotion was underpinned with a feeling of sadness and dread that Caleb would soon be far away. She did her work with absent-minded detachment and Sally was beginning to worry about her. The only thing that kept her grounded was her Bilbo. She managed to ride him a couple of times and happily let Sally ride him too. Sally had refused to charge her much for keeping him there, just a nominal fee. Carrie was now working for free and the advert for a new assistant had been in the local papers.

On the Wednesday Carrie decided she needed to confide in Sally about her fears. Both Sally and the lads knew Caleb was going away and were ready to support her. She hadn't told any of them how lacking in intimacy her and Caleb's relationship was.

In her mind this was by far the biggest hurdle she had had to cross so far. It was like she felt her marriage to Matt would be spoilt forever if she had sex with Caleb. It wasn't a rational thing, but a huge hang up she had gained somewhere along the line. She felt she didn't deserve to enjoy life fully, as Matt couldn't enjoy life any more. She had slowly let herself learn to enjoy other things but this was the final huge step to letting Matt go. It had become almost like a phobia of intimacy that she had to overcome. Since Monday's passion she knew she wanted to go there, she just didn't know how she would feel afterwards. And Caleb could not stay to kiss her tears away.

Sally was wonderful. Carrie poured her heart out about her deepest fears as Sally sat and held her hand. Once Carrie had told her everything Sally asked, "Do you love Caleb? Do you trust him? Do you see a future with him?"

Carrie nodded through her tears.

"Then you need to show him you feel those things, men see sex very differently to women, I think. It's a primaeval, deep-rooted thing about claiming their mate or something. Think about this step as being your gift to him. Not about your feelings, but about his. If you can think of it as a gift to him you can stop thinking about it being a betrayal of your old relationship. I know I never met

Matt but I'm sure nothing can take away what you had. You have let Matt go in so many ways but no one can change how much you loved him, even Caleb. That is history and no one can change history. History has huge value but it is not more valuable than the present. Let Caleb be your present, give him everything."

"Oh my god, Sally, how did you get so wise? I have been selfish in my grief, letting it taint my new relationship. I can do this for Caleb with willingness now I can see that."

"Grief is selfish, but you are not, you are ready to let your true self shine through, give him this last part of your heart, enjoy it."

"I will, thank you, Wise Sally."

"Soooo, can we get this painting finished now do you think?"

They both giggled and got to work.

I can see your smile Matt.

Chapter 18

The Gift

Thursday evening eventually arrived. Carrie had said her goodbyes to Sally and promised not to be too late in the morning. Caleb's flight was at 8am so she hoped to be a work for 10am. She had been shopping and treated herself to a new summery dress and some slightly less 'functional' underwear. She was quite relieved that Elver's few shops did not include anything too raunchy in their underwear departments, she wasn't feeling brave. She suddenly thought of contraception out of the blue. She was still on the pill, to balance her hormones, but she knew Caleb had had many partners – should she buy condoms to be safe? She decided she would and braved the chemists counter clutching a small box, whilst hoping the floor would swallow her up.

She had packed her bag and got herself showered and dressed by 5.30pm and was now calmly wearing a hole in the carpet with her pacing. Gregg and Dave were watching her with amusement, not realising quite why she was in such turmoil. At 5.45pm there was a knock at the door and Caleb's driver stood there smiling. "Hello my dear it doesn't seem five minutes since I was last in Elver, are you ready to go?" Carrie grabbed her bag, kissed the lads hastily and ran to the car before she lost her nerve. As she settled in the back of the car the driver said, "Caleb asked me to tell you he will be back at the hotel when we arrive, so I'm taking you straight there. He said all the film work was finished so you would have the whole evening to enjoy yourselves. Are you going anywhere nice?"

Carrie realised the only plans she knew about were not ones she could share with Caleb's driver. She laughed, "I have absolutely no idea what Caleb has planned, it will be a surprise."

The car pulled up at the front of the hotel. Carrie got out and thanked the driver, who had been good company, in his jolly, deferential way. He offered to see her in but she declined. She mounted the steps and entered the foyer, looking around at the beautiful décor. As she approached the front desk she heard her name called and Caleb appeared from a lift near the back of the foyer. She ran into his arms and he kissed her head. As she looked up he kissed her lips and smiled, "It's so good to see you sweetie, how was your day?"

"Oh Caleb, I'm so happy to be here – I missed your hugs." He hugged her again then walked them towards the lift with his arm tightly round her. The lift took them to the top floor and they entered his suite. "You got all your film stuff done then?" she asked as Caleb guided her to a sofa to sit.

"We did, all finished for me anyway. It's the editors and others who have to worry about the next bit." He sat down next to her with two cups of tea in his hands, passing hers as he spoke. "I know tea makes you relax so I had some sent up when the driver texted you were arriving. I thought you might appreciate it." She smiled and took a sip. "What shall we do this evening," asked Caleb, "would you like to go anywhere?" Carrie shook her head.

"I want us just to be together, I don't want to share you tonight."

"I like that idea," he said. As they sipped tea there was a tension between them that Carrie didn't recognise. It was almost as if the strong and confident Caleb was as nervous as she was. She hadn't expected that and it made her feel stronger somehow. She thought back to Sally's advice and decided he needed his gift now.

She leant across the sofa to Caleb and kissed his ear, just gently, he stilled. She moved closer and kissed his neck. He turned to her and caught her next kiss with one of his own, brushing lips on lips. As they kissed, Carrie softened her mouth to him and licked along his upper lip. He moaned softly as she gently nipped his lower lip with her teeth. His arms came around her and he deepened his kisses, exploring her mouth with his tongue. Their hands stilled as they kissed, enjoying the feel each other's mouths for a few blissful moments. Then Carrie slowly took her kisses lower, down his stubble, onto his gorgeous neck. He lounged back on the sofa and let her explore his throat with her lips. She pressed on down to the v of his shirt, gently breathing onto the kissed areas, heightening the sensation of where her lips had been. She started to open the buttons of his shirt, all the while kissing newly exposed flesh as she went lower. When she reached the line of his nipples she diverted and gently took one between her teeth. Caleb's low growl was almost animalistic as she nipped softly, bringing his skin to a hard peak.

Up till now Caleb had been watching her in wonder and enjoying the feeling of her exploration. Suddenly he could hold back no longer and his hands were all over her body. He grabbed her head and drew her roughly to his mouth. The kisses he gave were no longer gentle but hard and rough. She responded to his mouth with her own fire, kissing as if her life depended on it.

Caleb lifted her onto his lap and they kissed and licked, each in their own world of passion. Carrie ripped the rest of Caleb's buttons open and sucked at each of his nipples in turn, hearing that deep growl rumble from his chest again. Caleb grabbed the bottom hem of her dress and lifted it over her head in one rough movement leaving her breathless and exposed. His lips found her breasts through the material of her bra and the heat of his breath warmed her everywhere. With a slick and practised move, he undid the fastener and her bra fell away. His tiny gasp as he looked at her set her on fire. She pushed her chest up and towards him forcing him to claim her nipple in his mouth. She writhed on his lap as he nipped and sucked one breast and took the other in his hand, kneading and pulling till she thought she could take no more.

Her shoes were gone, having fallen off ages ago. She moved back and stood in front of him in just her panties. He looked for a moment drinking in her beautiful curves, then he stood, lifted her into his arms and carried her to the bedroom.

He laid her carefully onto the bed and stood over her. Within seconds he removed his torn shirt, his jeans and pants and stood over her again. She looked up at his bronzed chest and his wonderful hardness and gasped. He gently lowered himself beside her and put his arms around her.

"Oh Carrie, my darling girl, you are so beautiful. I need to slow down for a minute and just feel you near me. Sorry if I was too rough for a while there, you drove me crazy with need." He gently kissed her neck and sucked her soft earlobe, his hand running up and down her abdomen and chest. She turned her face and kissed his soft lips, running her tongue over them and gently pressing through into his mouth. They kissed long and slow, building a bond that was far more intimate than ever before.

"My lovely, lovely Carrie, can we stay here forever?" He deepened his kisses again, his breathing becoming harder and more passionate. She responded to his urgency and they breathed as one. His hands were searching now stroking her legs and her belly, waiting for her to invite him further. She opened up for him and his hands sought her wetness. He growled and stroked her, exploring and rubbing until she was panting and moaning. He pushed his finger deep inside her and she arched her back, clamping his finger as he thrust it into her. She called his name as her world fell apart and back together all in one amazing moment. His lips were on her mouth again gently kissing her as she returned to earth.

"I want you now Caleb, please!" she whispered holding his face and returning his kisses.

With a smile that again broke her in two and made her feel whole all at once, he moved his body over her and paused. "We can stop, even now, if you need to?" he said in a soft voice – you are in control." She smiled at him and lifted her hips, pushing him almost inside her. He moaned and pushed forward meeting her and entering her in one thrust. He looked deep into her eyes as he slowly increased the pace of his thrusts and felt and watched as she cried her way through another climax. Within a few more seconds he was joining her his head buried in her neck as the sensations hit him in waves of intense love and pleasure.

As they both slowly came down from their high, Caleb looked at Carrie. "I love you so much, there are no words to explain. Thank you for being you, thank you for letting me know it was time, I didn't know how you were feeling, I was nervous about assuming.........."

She placed her finger on his lips.

"My gift to you, and my gift to us," she smiled. They lay side by side for what felt like hours just holding one another and touching and stroking. She felt wonderful and so free, like a huge weight had been lifted, she felt nothing but love, no fear, no guilt, no Matt. She knew she could go forward and love Caleb as he deserved.

As Caleb's head cleared he suddenly looked worried. "Carrie I got so caught up in needing you I totally forgot about protection, I am so sorry my love." Carrie sat up and thought out loud, "I am on the pill, so no worries on that score, but...."

"I'm clean Carrie, I wouldn't have come near you

if I hadn't known that. I haven't touched anyone for over a year, I had myself tested 3 times in that year – all clear. I knew I wanted to change my behaviour back then and that was part of it – knowing I was clean. I haven't had sex without protection for years anyway, but I wanted to be sure. I am so sorry I am telling you this now and not before. I feel ashamed not to have thought of telling you."

"Caleb I have never been tested and I didn't think of it either, it's not just your responsibility. I have only ever slept with Matt and I believe he only ever slept with me. We have taken the risk and it is a very small risk, let's not worry about it. I even got brave and bought some condoms to bring tonight, and I still did not remember to use them. We must be like horny teenagers!"

"You bought condoms, isn't that the horny boy's job? I have some too." Caleb giggled.

"Hey, I'm a twenty-first century girl, I can buy condoms, I wasn't even embarrassed – Much!"

They hugged and Caleb pulled the duvet over them as it was getting cool. "We should think about eating," he said, kissing her. "Only if we can think about being back here soon after." Carrie murmured from under the duvet. Caleb laughed, "Room service it is then." Much later, after a meal that Carrie couldn't really remember, apart from the syrup,

179

which they might have shared a little too enthusiastically, they were once again laying in each other's arms. "I can't believe you are going away in the morning," said Carrie. "I feel like I've just found you, and now I am losing you."

"You will never lose me now, Carrie," said Caleb softly. "I'll always come home to you."

"Can we talk every day, do you promise to make time?"

"Every day, I promise."

"Are you going to stay with your parents or do they live a long way from where you're filming?"

"Far enough thank goodness, I love them dearly but we get on best when the visits are short. I will try to see them a few times and I will tell them about my fiancée and our new home. When you come to visit we'll meet up with them."

"I'd like that, as long as we get time alone as well!" Carrie grinned and ran a finger around his nipple.

"Don't worry on that score," he grinned back, "parents will be a long way down the list of priorities if I have my way."

"We should get some sleep now," Carrie said. "You have a long journey tomorrow."

"I can sleep on the plane," he whispered huskily, taking Carrie in his arms once more. They made love slowly and gently this time, learning more about each other and making memories to tide them over during their time apart.

You are fading Matt, be happy my love.........

Epilogue

The next morning was a rush of waking, packing and scrambling into the car. They hadn't woken until reception rang the room to say their car was waiting. The race across London to get to the airport was tense and they only just arrived with enough time to hastily hug and kiss before Caleb dashed to priority boarding, shouting back that he would phone when he arrived. Suddenly Carrie was alone.

The car was waiting for her, so she made her way back outside and they started the journey back to Elver. Even the driver's banter couldn't keep her mood from dropping like a stone. She reached into her purse for a tissue and her hand brushed something hidden in the pocket. She pulled it out and found it was the dried flower she had kept from Caleb's first present to her all those weeks ago. As she held it, the need to cry slowly left her. She had come so far since then, why was she sad? She had gone from having a gaping hole in her life, barely surviving, to having the most wonderful partner, a beautiful horse and the future she never thought she would have.

She carefully replaced the flower and thought

about the farm. Thought about Caleb and all the animals they could save together. She must ring Mr Bernard and see if he could cut and bale the rest of the hay for them so they had feed ready for next winter. If he could not, she would find a contractor to do it. She should get some quotes for making the outbuildings watertight until they decided how to renovate them. She would see if Andrew or his father could recommend someone.

The next few months would pass in a flash, she had so much to plan. Every night she could talk the plans through with Caleb and keep him involved in any decisions. She would discuss the future of her home in Elver with the lads – maybe they would buy it? They could certainly stay there renting as long as they wanted.

By the time the car was nearing Elver, she realised her life was perfect, no need for tears. Crying was a habit she would be happy to break. She could wait patiently for Caleb as he had waited for her. Their future spread out before her, and it was amazing.

I'm here waiting for you Caleb..........

THE END

Printed in Great Britain
by Amazon

61842596R00107